THE PRISUNER OF BHOPAL

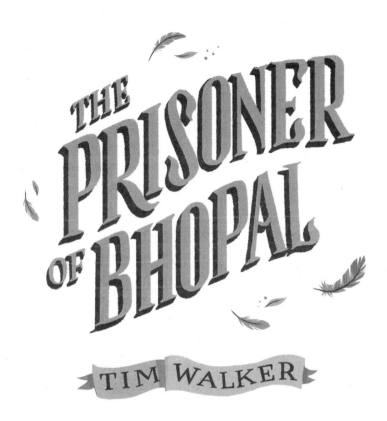

THE PRISONER OF BHOPAL

TIM WALKER

A

ANDERSEN PRESS

First published in 2024 by
Andersen Press Limited
20 Vauxhall Bridge Road, London SW1V 2SA, UK
Vijverlaan 48, 3062 HL Rotterdam, Nederland
www.andersenpress.co.uk

2 4 6 8 10 9 7 5 3 1

British Library Cataloguing in Publication Data available.

ISBN 978 1 83913 373 2

Printed and bound in Great Britain by Clays Ltd, Elcograf S.p.A.

For Jo

Beneath the starlight of an Indian sky, a boy is running. Others follow him as he twists and turns through the city's streets and alleyways, one clean breath ahead of the poisonous gas cloud which is pursuing them. Seen from above the cloud might seem unstoppable – which indeed it is – like a wave breaking over the seashore. But look closer and there is another story. For just as seawater breaks around every rock and pebble in its path, so every bush, every telegraph pole, every tumbledown shack and temple guides this deathly wind along a course which no one can see.

No one except the boy.

He alone knows where the cloud will falter, where it will speed up or roll sideways, or spiral skyward in the swirling updraft between opposing obstacles. He turns one last time and hurtles towards the advancing cloud. Moments later, as he knew it would, it parts, drawn aside like a pair of sickly yellow curtains to reveal the clear, safe air beyond. But the boy does not reach the other side. At the last moment he falls, and as the dust around him shudders under a thousand stampeding feet, the curtains begin to close.

1

1984: A Hurricane Arrives

On his tenth birthday a hurricane tore the roof off Amil Gujar's house and sucked him into the sky. At least, that is how it felt to him.

He had begun the day as he began every day, perched on top of the telegraph pole which stood outside the tiny two-roomed house which he shared with his mother and father, his two younger brothers and his grandparents. No one in his street owned a telephone, nor had ever used one. But that did not matter to Amil. With his long spidery limbs he would climb the wooden pole every morning before breakfast, and every afternoon after school, staring into the wind for so long that his thick black hair had become permanently pushed back from his face, like the branches of a windswept tree. This was Amil's favourite place. From the top he could see the ancient domed temples of Bhopal, rising like giant golden onions from the old part of the city, and trace the black telegraph cable as it drew long low scoops across the sky towards him. Then, as it skimmed over his head, his eyes would follow the line all the way to the pesticide plant, which lay half a mile in the opposite direction. He never tired of gazing at its towering silver storage tanks, and imagining himself working there one day, alongside his father and his uncle Ravi – his beloved Chachaji. Until then, with a turn of his head he could see India's past and its future, and he was precisely where he wanted to be, right in the middle.

On any normal morning he would have stayed aloft long enough to watch his uncle walk from his house nearby, which he shared with his wife, Maya, and their two young daughters, to collect his father for work. As he approached, his uncle would look up and wave to him. Then his father would emerge from the house wearing his blue overalls and white safety helmet, and together they would set off for the pesticide plant. But this morning his father had not gone to work. Today was a special day. The aroma of warm aloo paratha – freshly baked by his mother in honour of his birthday – drew him back down to earth, and he rushed indoors. His brothers and his grandparents were still soundly asleep in the back room, but his mother and father were waiting for him, stiff and unsmiling. Amil gave his mother a huge birthday grin. She crouched down and hugged him so tightly that he could barely breathe. Then she held him firmly by the shoulders and looked deep into his eyes, as though she wished to climb into his head and hug him from the inside.

'Amil, there is something very important which your father and I have to tell you . . .' But before she could continue, there was a knock at the door. Amil broke away and opened it.

The hurricane had arrived.

2
A Matter of Honour

The shape of a man filled the doorway, black and faceless within a halo of morning light.

'Today is the day, Mrs Gujar,' the shape said.

Amil's heart almost burst with joy. He looked back at his mother, expecting her face to reveal the delivery of a special gift, or some other birthday treat. But she did not look back at him. Her eyes were fixed on the stranger.

'You are too early!' he heard his father cry.

The man stepped into the room. 'Have you not told him yet? You knew this day would come.' Without warning he grabbed Amil's arm and pulled him towards the open doorway. 'I will explain the matter to the boy myself.' Amil screamed and reached for his mother, and she for him. But his father held her back. Amil expected her to break free and launch herself at the man like a lioness protecting her cub, to bite and claw at his flesh until he let him go. But his mother merely hugged her stomach, groaning, as his father held her. They did nothing to save him. They let the man drag him outside without a fight, as if it were the right and proper thing to do.

Amil kicked and screamed and scratched and bit and tried every way he could to free himself. But the man merely tightened his grip, dragging him further and further down the street, away from his home and his family. None of his neighbours came to his aid. Instead, mothers ushered their children indoors whilst their husbands looked on, some even nodding their approval. Everyone in Bhopal appeared to know what was happening to Amil. And why. Everyone, that is, except Amil himself. As they turned the corner the man lifted Amil off the ground and slung him over his shoulder like a sack of flour. He quickened his pace, as Amil continued to scream and lash out with his fists, pummelling the sweat-soaked shirt stretched across the stranger's back like the skin of a plump, over-ripe tomato. But the man appeared barely to notice, and marched on.

Soon, Amil no longer recognised where they were. Through the acid haze of his tears he could see little more than the man's cracked heels in his sandals, bicycle wheels spinning by, cattle hooves and cartwheels and, occasionally, the outstretched hand of a beggar. The man turned into a market, and the view changed. As Amil continued to pound on the back of his abductor, images flashed in front of him: rows of sandals laid out according to size and colour, precarious pyramids of limes and lemons, pumpkins and potatoes, coconuts, cauliflowers and cabbages, the threadbare backs of half-starved dogs weaving their way through a forest of legs, as a thousand people jostled through the narrow alleyways, kicking up dust. Amil looked up at the passing faces, hoping that one might recognise him and return him to his family. But no one even glanced at him.

They turned a corner, leaving the shops and market stalls behind them. The streets were wider now, but with few stone buildings. Instead they were lined with hundreds of tumbledown shacks made from scraps of wood and rusty corrugated sheeting, crammed together like rotten teeth in a mouth that was too small for them. Rising out of this sea of deprivation, the crumbling facades of two stone buildings stood facing each other across the street, decaying remnants of more prosperous times. The man headed for the double doors belonging to the workshop on the left, above which stretched the words *Kumar & Sons Printers* in flaky, sun-bleached lettering. By the time they reached them, all Amil's tears had leaked into the dirt and his throat felt as though it were full of broken glass. He stopped screaming. There was a jangling of keys, then the discordant creak of one of the doors as it opened. His captor carried him inside, then locked the door behind them and dropped Amil to the ground.

'Sit there,' he commanded. He pointed to a white plastic chair, similar to those which lined the streets outside every tea house in Bhopal. As Amil slid into the chair, the man drew up another, and sat facing him in the semi-darkness. He took a handkerchief from his pocket, and ran it over the wide hairless channel which stretched from his forehead to the back of his neck, dabbing sweat. For a few moments he stared at Amil, drumming the arm of the chair with his stubby fingers. Finally, he leaned forward.

'Listen to me, boy,' he said, waving a finger in Amil's face. 'My name is Mr Kumar, and I am a respectable businessman. I am not kidnapping you, do you understand? This is a matter of family honour.'

Amil said nothing. Perhaps he was still asleep, dreaming. Or, perhaps this was what his mother meant when she told him not to let his imagination carry him away. He pinched his arm hard. Mr Kumar did not disappear.

'Do you know what honour is, boy?' Amil nodded, weakly, so Mr Kumar continued: 'It means doing what is right, so that you may hold your head up proudly among your fellows. There is also such a thing as family honour. Do you believe in the honour of the Gujar family?' Amil nodded again, this time more confidently. 'Sadly, your great-grandfather did not. He brought death and ruin to our family, and heaped shame on his own like a mountain of elephant dung. Look around you, boy. This was once a thriving business, set in the heart of a prosperous neighbourhood. Now, the place is falling to pieces and we are marooned in a sea of riff-raff. And it is all the fault of your great-grandfather.'

'What . . . what did he do?' Amil croaked.

Mr Kumar's mouth tightened as though he had just bitten into a rotten almond. 'Your great-grandfather left three of my ancestors to die on the battlefield – that is what he did. He betrayed them. He was a coward; a traitor; a deserter; a disgrace to every Indian soldier that fought and died for the honour of this country. The pain that gutless, low-caste Gujar inflicted that day has seeped like a poison through generations of our family, bringing with it nothing but bad luck and hardship. That is why you are here.' He paused to wipe more beads of sweat from his forehead. 'A debt is owed, you see. As we businessmen say, the books must be balanced. For without balance in all things, the world would tilt on its axis and spin out of control.' Mr Kumar returned the handkerchief to his pocket.

'But how can I repay this debt?' asked Amil.

Mr Kumar frowned. 'You cannot properly repay it, unless you can bring back the dead. All you can do is repay a small fraction of it, like your father before you. The stench of shame that clings to your family will take a thousand years to wash away. And hard work is the only soap. That is why, for the next eight years, you will sleep in here by night, and by day you will fold paper for our customers. And when you are not folding paper, you will fetch, you will carry, you will clean, you will stand on your head in a bucket of chicken guts, if I command it. And one day, when your first-born son is ten years old, he will do the same. Drop by drop, generation by generation, the Gujars will continue to atone for the tidal wave of grief that your great-grandfather unleashed on our family all those years ago. That is how the debt is to be repaid. Is that clear?'

Before Amil could answer there was a knock on the door. Mr Kumar heaved himself out of his chair and opened it. Amil shielded his eyes as a shaft of light struck him in the face, like the sudden glare of an interrogator's lamp. A boy, older and taller than Amil, and with curly hair stretching over his frayed collar, stepped inside, carrying a broom over his shoulder. He strutted confidently towards Amil, his chest puffed out, his shirt-sleeves rolled up to his armpits to accentuate his muscles. Amil drew his knees up to his chest and pressed himself into the back of his chair. The boy circled him, tapping the end of the broom handle against the stone floor with the slow, rhythmic menace of a ticking bomb.

'This is my son, Jalesh,' Mr Kumar explained proudly. 'You will do as he says.'

'He is shaking like a coward, Pappa,' Jalesh observed.

'He is a Gujar,' his father replied, 'what do you expect?' Mr Kumar looked at his watch. 'You should be on your way to school. Where is your school bag?'

His son ignored him. Instead, he crouched down in front of Amil. 'I hope you like rats,' he said, 'because they are all that is left in the workshop now, thanks to your family.'

'School, Jalesh!'

The boy turned angrily to his father. 'What is the point of school, if already my life is cursed by this boy and his family!' He sent the broom clattering to the floor in front of Amil. 'One end is for the rats, the other is for the cockroaches. When you are not fighting them off, you can sweep the floor with it. And you will keep out of my way if you know what is good for you.' As he strode out of the workshop, he called back to his father: 'And I am not going to school today.'

Mr Kumar jabbed a finger at Amil.

'See what you have done!' He turned to leave. As he reached the door, Amil leaped up and tried to make his escape. But Mr Kumar blocked his way, batting him aside with his hand, before slamming the door shut behind him. The key turned in the lock. Amil jumped back to his feet and launched himself at the door, kicking it and pounding it with his fists.

'None of it is true! I do not believe you! Let me out. *Let me out!*'

Mr Kumar called to him through the rattling woodwork: 'Control yourself, boy. You will stay in there until you calm down.'

But Amil did not calm down. He had to get back to his mother and father. All morning he pounded on the door, calling for help. And when his hands were so bruised and swollen that he could no longer do that, he picked up the broom and began battering the door with the end of the handle. But no one came. So, he turned his attention inside, examining the workshop for any means of escape. The room was long and narrow. There were just two windows, one each side of the double doors, both crudely boarded over with planks. Gaps in the woodwork allowed Amil to view bright slivers of bobbing heads or shuffling feet in the street beyond. From those same gaps, blades of dust-filled light sliced through the gloom and cast themselves like luminous prison bars on the wall behind him. Amil tried to dislodge one of the boards but it was nailed tightly to the frame from the outside. The only other light in the workshop came from two small ventilation grilles, both beyond arm's reach, secured by screws set solid with rust. At one end of the room a set of wooden steps, little more than a ladder, led to a hatch in the ceiling.

The steps were rotten, and halfway up several were missing entirely, but compared to a telegraph pole they were an easy climb. Amil soon managed to scramble up to the hatch. That too was locked. From the top he began scouring the workshop for anything that might help him escape. But the room was all but bare, with just a few empty cardboard boxes, a long trestle table and a few more of the white plastic chairs. He scanned the floor for trapdoors, drain covers, anything that might lead to the outside. But there was nothing.

Instead, he noticed that even in the half-light the stone floor was splattered with black ink, as though an airborne army of suicidal cockroaches had dive-bombed into the stone. Framed by this inky carnage, several rectangular patches of stone remained unblemished; ghostly footprints of the machines that once stood there. Finally, in the corner just below him, stood an old white sink, supported on four rusting legs and covered in a million tiny cracks, like the veins on a dried-up leaf. Suddenly, Amil realised how thirsty he was. He jumped down and turned on the tap, but nothing but a hiss came from the spout. He tipped his head forward and tapped the pipework hard with his hand in an attempt to coax one or two droplets on to his tongue. But his mouth remained dry. As he straightened up, he heard a noise and turned. There, at the foot of the door, was a metal plate on which stood a plastic beaker of water and a roti. He ran over to the door and called out: 'Hello. *Hello!*' But there was no answer. Around the edge of the beaker, he noticed several small floury fingerprints. He raised it to his nose and sniffed the water, before gulping it down in one go. Then, as he chewed the bread, he examined the small hatch through which the tray had been placed, quickly concluding that even *he* was not thin enough to squeeze through it. Clearly, he would have to find some other means of escape. But escape, he would. Because he knew that none of what Mr Kumar had said was true. And his father would tell him so.

3

A New Pair of Sandals

Amil's hands and feet ached. He had been balanced over the workshop door for almost two hours, having climbed into position as soon as the first streaks of morning light had pierced the window boards. With his feet pressed tight against the top of the doorframe and his hands gripping one of the crossbeams that supported the attic above, all he could do now was wait.

He had not slept at all that night. Instead, he had spent every moment searching for a way out of the workshop. One of the plastic chairs stood on the trestle table beneath the ventilation grill, which he had tried to loosen. Small piles of loose plaster and splinters of wood lay around the perimeter of the room, the product of several hours clawing at any weakness in the walls and boarded-up windows. Nothing had worked, and by the time the cockerels crowed over Bhopal, the tips of his fingers were worn and bloodied. They had not been designed to unscrew rusty bolts, or remove nails, or dig through brickwork. But

16

then a plan had popped into his head. And now he was ready.

He heard a door open on the opposite side of the street. Then a single pair of heavy, shuffling footsteps. Good: Mr Kumar was alone, he would not have to outrun Jalesh. He looked down at the seven-foot drop to the ground. A key rattled in the lock and he flexed his knees, ready to jump. Suddenly, light flooded in through the open doorway. For a moment Mr Kumar stood there, his shiny head already glistening with sweat just inches below Amil's feet. The workshop looked empty to him, yet he knew the boy must be in there somewhere, lurking like a coward in the shadows. He stepped inside, squinting into the darkness. One pace. Two. Amil jumped down into a crouch behind him. By the time Mr Kumar turned, he had sprung through the doorway and run halfway down the street.

He did not look back to see Mr Kumar puffing after him. At the end of the street, he turned left, then right down a narrow alleyway, ducking under clothes lines and scattering chickens. He stopped at the next junction, uncertain which way to turn, aware that if he made the wrong decision he might run straight into the arms of Mr Kumar. He looked up, searching for the black telephone cable which he knew would guide him home. Then he saw it: a thin black line drawn over the end of the alley to his right. He raced towards it. Around the next corner he found the first telegraph pole. Quickly, he registered the direction of the cable leading from it and set off again. From pole to pole he ran, zigzagging through the streets and alleyways, looking up after every few paces to check that the cable was still in view. Soon, he began to recognise his neighbourhood, and then his street and, finally, the telegraph pole outside his house. He ran straight indoors.

What he saw inside convinced him, more than ever, that he was in the middle of a terrible nightmare from which, surely, he must soon awake. For there in his house, tucking into their breakfast, was a family that was not his. Strangers. The man jumped to his feet.

'What is the meaning of this? How dare you burst into my house. Get out!'

Amil ignored him, and ran into the back room, spinning around dizzily in search of familiar things. But nothing was the same. His favourite picture, of Vayu, God of the Wind, which used to hang on the wall above his sleeping mat, had been replaced by a photograph of a famous Indian cricketer. Every picture in the house was different. A further shock greeted him as he returned to the main room where, as on his birthday, the shape of a man filled the doorway, black and faceless within a halo of morning light. This time, Amil would not be caught. He ran at the man, diving through his open legs to escape his grasp. He landed at the foot of the telegraph pole, and had almost reached the top before the man called out his name. Amil looked down, and finally recognised his pursuer.

'Chachaji!'

His uncle removed his safety helmet and tucked it under his arm. 'I was on my way to work. What is going on? You should be with Mr Kumar.'

'Where are my mother and father?' Amil pleaded.

His uncle hesitated. 'Your father lost his job at the pesticide plant, Amil. They have moved to the countryside to become farmers – it was arranged many weeks ago.'

Amil hugged the pole, as if it were the only thing in the world that was real. 'Why did they not tell me they were going away? And about my great-grandfather? And about Mr Kumar?'

'They were planning to tell you everything yesterday, Amil, then take you to Mr Kumar's before leaving for the country. No one thought he would be cruel enough to take you away so early in the morning.'

Amil's eyes filled with tears.

'They should have told me before.'

Uncle Ravi sighed. 'And if they had told you a month ago, or a year ago, would you have been happy even for a single moment, knowing that you were to be parted from them?'

Amil shook his head.

'And would you be any happier now?'

A tear rolled down Amil's cheek, and fell like a solitary raindrop to the ground.

'No,' he replied.

'That is the reason they did not tell you,' his uncle explained. 'They wanted you to be happy until the moment you had to leave, even though behind their smiles they were not. They have suffered the pain of losing you from the day you were born, and quietly prepared you for it. That is why you are strong and resourceful, and why they gave you extra lessons at home to make sure that you can read and write. Because from today, there will be no more school for you, Amil. Only work for Mr Kumar and his family. That is to be your life now.'

'I am not going back!' Amil cried. 'And if you take me there, I will run away again.'

'You can run away as often as you like, Amil, but our family shame is like a prison from which there is no escape. Running will only bring us further dishonour and increase our debt to the Kumars. This, in turn, you will be passing on to your own son, and to his son after that. It is as Mr Kumar has told you.'

Amil hugged the pole tighter. 'Then I will never get married, and I will never have children.'

Uncle Ravi shook his head. 'We must atone for the

crimes of our ancestor, Amil. Otherwise, our family name will be shamed for all eternity. One day, you will be reunited with your family. I promise. Until then, you must continue to restore the honour of the Gujar name as your father did before you. Do you understand?'

Amil nodded weakly. Yet he did not want to return to Mr Kumar's. Surely there was another way. 'Can I repay the debt with money?' he asked.

Before his uncle could answer, Mr Kumar arrived in a heaving cloud of puff and sweat. 'Money?' he roared. 'This debt . . . cannot be . . . repaid with money!'

'Not even a million rupees?' asked Amil.

For a split-second Mr Kumar hesitated. 'And do you intend to break into the bank of Bhopal, may I ask? To rob the citizens of their money as your great-grandfather robbed the Kumar brothers of their lives?'

Amil shook his head. 'I would earn it honestly. I promise.'

By now a small crowd had gathered to watch the early morning entertainment. Mr Kumar found himself centre stage, playing the aggrieved party in a piece of improvised street theatre. Perhaps some humour was called for.

'If ever you earn a million rupees,' he replied, revelling in the attention, 'I will not only release your family from their debt, I will dance naked through the streets of Bhopal . . . wearing a chicken on my head!' He acknowledged a ripple of applause for his generous and light-hearted riposte. 'But,' he added foolishly, showing Amil the palm of his hand, 'unless you come down now, the debt will be paid by your backside.'

Uncle Ravi clasped his forehead. Amil's father had never lifted a finger to his son. As he feared it would, the mere mention of a beating served only to tighten Amil's grip around the top of the telegraph pole.

And that is where he stayed. For seven days and seven nights, his arms and legs remained locked together in a tight knot, as he clung to every last moment of his freedom as if it were his dying breath. Whilst Uncle Ravi and his former neighbours took turns to watch him, and Mr Kumar returned each day to unwittingly sabotage their attempts to coax him down, a small community grew up around the foot of the pole. Small campfires were lit. Aromatic smoke wafted upwards as the spectators cooked all kinds of mouth-watering titbits with which to tempt Amil down from his perch. Conversation flowed. Words of wisdom were exchanged on matters of honour, and bets taken on how long Amil could remain aloft.

'He will tire soon enough – look at those skinny arms. Mark my words, he will be back on the ground by sunset.'

'Perhaps we should set fire to the telegraph pole,' someone joked. 'That will get him down soon enough.'

'Or grease it with cooking oil and watch him slide down!' suggested another.

Everyone had an opinion, yet they all agreed that Amil would come down when he was hungry or thirsty. But all of them were wrong. Neither hunger nor thirst could budge him. Some onlookers reported that on more than one occasion, a large grey heron had flown up from Bhopal's Upper Lake to perch beside Amil, and feed him small fish directly from its long, dagger-like beak. Others said that a miniature monsoon cloud – the only cloud of any description to be found in the skies above Bhopal that week – opened up above him to quench his thirst whenever he stretched out his tongue. But one thing Amil could not do was stay awake for ever, and as the sun set on the seventh day his sagging eyelids finally closed, and the human knot at the top of the telegraph pole unravelled. His uncle was there to catch him, and would tell Amil later that as he fell, a sudden gust of wind had, as if by some divine sorcery, billowed beneath him to cushion his descent, and deliver him safely into his outstretched arms.

That night Uncle Ravi carried Amil back to the workshop. The door was open so he set Amil down on one of the chairs. Then he stepped outside to talk to Mr Kumar, who had emerged from the house. Amil listened bleary-eyed to the hiss and murmur and intermittent raising of their voices, not quite sure whether they were real or inside his head. But then his uncle returned and sat on the floor in front of him.

Even though less than a year in age separated them, Uncle Ravi was very different from his older brother, Amil's father. Whereas Amil's father was thin and wiry, with stooped shoulders, Ravi was heavyset, with strong arms and a straight back. He sported a thick handlebar moustache, the ends of which he would twist into finely curled points between dampened fingertips every morning. Unlike his brother's thinning grey hair, Ravi's was dark and dense, with the permanent imprint of his work helmet running round it like a halo. And indeed, if not saintly, he was certainly a good man and never forgot that, had he been born before his brother, it is he who would have inherited the Gujar family debt of honour.

'I want to see my mother and father,' said Amil. '*Please*, Chachaji.'

His uncle removed his helmet and placed it beside him. 'I am sorry, Amil. As Mr Kumar has explained, your parents cannot see you, or even contact you. They must feel the loss of a son. That is part of the debt which also must be paid.' He leaned forward to squeeze Amil's hand. 'Only I am permitted to visit you, but I promise to bring you news of them once a week or whenever I can, even though Mr Kumar will not like it.'

More tears rolled down Amil's cheeks. His uncle dabbed them away with his sleeve.

'I often sneaked in to visit your father when he worked here,' he said, looking around the workshop. 'You see those bare patches of stone? The workshop used to pulsate under the noise of the machines that stood on them. Once upon a time, fine books of poetry were produced here, some for the princess of Bhopal herself. Their words were forged out of molten metal on a huge clattering machine that was like a miniature metalwork foundry. After they cooled, another machine would print those words on to fine textured paper which yet more machines would fold and cut and stitch until, hey presto, the words of India's finest poets, bound for all eternity, lay nestling in one's hands. That was long, long ago, when Bhopal was ruled by princesses, and poetry was sung in the streets. When your father began work here, those machines still filled the room, printing leaflets and posters for customers across the city. But by the time he left, when he was eighteen, only half of them remained. And now they are all gone. I hear that folding paper by hand is all that Kumar and Sons does now.' He gestured towards the boxes of leaflets which had arrived in Amil's absence, and which sat beside the trestle table, awaiting his novice fingers. 'And to think Mr Kumar still struts around calling himself a businessman.'

'Where did all the machines go?' asked Amil.

His uncle shrugged. 'Your father says that Mr Kumar sold them to pay off his gambling debts, and that his parents died from the shame. I am sure he blames our family for that too. And for the monsoons. And for the big hairy pimple on the end of his nose.'

To his uncle's great relief, Amil smiled. 'Do you know what is up there?' he asked, pointing to the hatch in the ceiling.

'I have no idea,' his uncle replied. 'Your father lived in this room for eight years and he says that only Mr Kumar ever ventured into the attic. And he always kept it locked. We used to wonder whether he had some deep, dark secret hidden in there. That reminds me . . .' He pulled a flat, crumpled package from his back pocket and placed it in Amil's hands. 'It is a birthday present from your mother and father.'

Amil plucked numbly at the crumpled newspaper in which it was wrapped. Inside was a pair of sandals.

'Your parents deliberately chose a pair several sizes too big for you, and told the shoemaker to add extra stitching so that they will last many years.' Uncle Ravi removed Amil's old sandals and slipped on the new ones, fastening them on the tightest notch. Even so, they were a very loose fit. 'Look after them, Amil. By the time they are a perfect fit, you will be a man, and free to leave here.' He reached into his breast pocket. 'And this is from me.' He handed Amil a small white torch proudly bearing the name of the pesticide plant along its side. 'Mr Kumar is notoriously mean; if you do not wish to spend your evenings in the dark, you will need this.'

Amil flashed the torch on and off.

'Use it sparingly, I will bring replacement batteries to you whenever I can,' his uncle told him. He leaned forward and hugged Amil tight. 'I must go now. If you promise me that you will not run away again, Mr Kumar has agreed to forget the matter of the telegraph pole.'

Amil nodded. 'I promise,' he said.

And so it was settled. There would be no beating. At least, not that night.

4

Nine Floury Fingers

The following day, Amil was woken by a loud, rhythmic squeaking, like a rat chanting its morning prayers. Instinctively, he pulled his legs up on to the chair in which he had slept, and scanned the semi-darkness for anything with a tail. Soon, he realised that the squeak was coming from the street. And it was growing louder. For a moment it stopped as a key turned in the lock. Amil stood up, shielding his eyes against the autumn sun as the workshop doors swung open. Mr Kumar strode inside, pulling a small wooden cart behind him, the sides of which bore the name *Kumar & Sons* in lettering so chipped and faded that Amil could barely read it. Carelessly, Mr Kumar let the heavy metal handle crash to the ground an inch from Amil's toes. He gripped his arm. 'Come with me,' he said.

He led Amil over the street to the house opposite. Aside from the workshop, it was the only building in the street made of brick. Even so, with barely a tile on its roof that was not broken, and brickwork that crumbled to the touch like parched earth, the house appeared as dilapidated as the tumbledown shacks propped up on either side of it. Mr Kumar ushered Amil to the doorway. 'Stand there and do not move,' he said. He stepped inside the house. 'Chunni, come here. I have brought the boy.'

Amil was expecting to meet Mr Kumar's wife. Instead, a girl, slightly shorter but more strongly built than him, emerged from behind some bead curtains. Her long black hair was arranged in a single plait down her back, her flour-covered hands held upright in front of her as though she were wearing a pair of white sock puppets. A small floury rolling pin protruded from a pocket in the front of her dress. She looked Amil up and down, unsmiling. Another mouth to feed. Unlike her brother who attended school, or at least pretended to, Chunni had never set foot in a classroom, and could neither read nor write. Nevertheless, behind her slightly narrowed eyes, currently fixed thoughtfully on Amil, there lay a fine business brain. Amil noticed her tapping the air silently with a floury forefinger, as if she were counting on an invisible abacus. After a few seconds, she stopped. 'He has good, slim paper-folding fingers, Pappaji. When he is properly trained he will not only earn his keep, but I will have time to spend on more profitable activities. Perhaps, I can also . . .' She hesitated. '. . . go to school.'

Her father batted her suggestion away like a fly.

'You are not going anywhere,' he told her. 'If you have any extra time you will spend it here, fulfilling your household duties.'

Jalesh appeared from the back room, clutching his school bag.

'Like licking our sandals clean,' he joked, 'and catching the cockroaches.'

As Jalesh pushed past Amil, his father reached over to give him a playful clip across the ear.

'Such a joker,' he said, before calling after him: 'It is a shame your sister has no sense of humour!' He ran his fingers over the door lintel, observing with tutting disapproval the layer of dust that accumulated on his fingertips. 'You have no idea of cleanliness either,' he said, holding up a fingertip for Chunni's inspection. 'This place is getting more like a cowshed every day. What would people say if they saw this filth? Your mother would be ashamed of you.'

Chunni glanced at Amil.

'Do not expect the boy to help you clean. When he is not folding paper, you can find other work for him to do, but not in this house. I will not have a Gujar under my roof.'

Chunni nodded obediently, then wiped a bead of sweat from her forehead with the back of a floury hand, inadvertently dusting the hair around her temple. The flecks of white reminded Amil of his mother, and for a moment he could almost see her, as though she were trying to drag him out of the nightmare in which he found himself. Mr Kumar prodded him sharply in the back. 'Say something, then. Even a low-caste boy like you should have some manners.' But Amil did not want to say anything. He did not wish to make this nightmare more real by taking part in it, or by adding detail to the characters inside it. He wanted them to remain mysterious and unclear, like distant shapes in a thick fog, so that one day he might awake to find the fog lifted, and his real life revealed underneath. And yet, before he could stop it, a question had found its way on to his tongue.

'How old are you?' he said.

Amil's ear stung from the back of Mr Kumar's hand. He cupped it in pain.

'Did I say you could start a conversation? What do you think this is, some kind of social gathering? A normal, civilised "hello" will do.'

With tears welling up in his eyes, Amil pressed his hands together and bowed his head slightly to Chunni.

'Hello,' he said quietly. He did not hear Chunni's reply. Mr Kumar was already pulling him back across the street by his arm. But, as he glanced over his shoulder, she was standing in the doorway. And as their eyes met, she held up nine floury fingers.

Inside the workshop, Mr Kumar tapped one of the wheels of the cart with his foot. 'The wheels need oiling,' he said, 'especially this one.' He hesitated for a moment, before pulling a bunch of keys from his pocket. 'No one has been in the attic since the steps rotted, so there is probably an old can of oil still inside. When you find it, be sure to come straight back. I do not want you nosing around up there.'

Amil pressed himself against the wall as Mr Kumar strode past him to the ladder, climbing as far as the missing rungs would allow, before reaching up to unlock the hatch. Amil looked longingly through the open doors to the street beyond – the street that would lead to another street, that would lead to a road, that would lead to a country track, that would lead him to his family. But he did not move. He had given his word that he would not run away again. And he had been taught always to keep his word. Mr Kumar stepped back on to the floor.

'I will be along later to teach you how to fold paper. In the meantime, get busy.' Then the double doors closed and a key turned in the lock. Clearly, for Mr Kumar, Amil's word was not enough.

Amil climbed up to the hatch and pushed it open on its creaking hinges. As the heavy door swung down inside the attic the floor shuddered, and twenty years of dust erupted into the air. Amil bowed his head as it settled around him. Then he shook the dust out of his hair and peered gingerly inside. Satisfied that an army of rats was not lying in wait for him, he lifted himself up. The floorboards were dry and splintery, with rusty nails protruding wherever half-hearted repairs had been carried out. Amil was glad of his new oversized sandals, despite stumbling several times on the uneven boards. Above him was a pitched corrugated iron roof, into which was set a skylight, bereft of glass except for a few stubborn shards clinging like shark's teeth to its rotten frame. A sheet of plastic, once clear but now brittle and yellowed with age, was tacked loosely over the hole, bathing the attic in a sickly mustard-coloured light, like a faded old photograph. Sitting beneath the skylight was a wooden trunk. The dustsheets that once concealed it had long ago rotted and fallen away, exposing it to the relentless drip, drip, drip of successive monsoon rains seeping in through the plastic above. Over time, the huge padlock intended to secure its contents from prying eyes had rusted to almost nothing.

The attic air hung heavy with heat. At one end of the room sat dozens of discarded tins of black ink, stacked precariously against the wall. Alongside them lay a huge pile of blackened cleaning rags, their ink-encrusted creases set firm with age, like the folds of a miniature mountain range. An empty box of rat poison lay on the floor among them, gnawed open by its victims, whose bodies lay shrivelled and rigid amongst the cloth and shredded cardboard. At the other end of the room the wall was lined with shelves, each sagging under the weight of countless jars, bottles and tins containing the pungent remains of a derelict printing business – more inks and oils, spirits and solvents, and numerous pots of bookbinding glue. Either through carelessness or the passage of time, their fumes seeped out through half-closed lids, leaking caps or cracked plastic, lacing the air with sharp, acrid smells which prickled the inside of Amil's nose before swirling up into his head, leaving him slightly giddy.

He found a small rectangular tin of oil on one of the shelves and returned to the cart. No sooner had he finished squeezing oil through the nozzle on to each of the wheel's axles – a job he had seen his father do when mending his bicycle – than Mr Kumar reappeared. Amil's new career as a paper-folder was about to begin.

5

A Successful Business

'If you are to become our new paper-folding machine, there are some things you must learn,' Mr Kumar told Amil. 'Kumar and Sons has a reputation for quality that must be upheld. Is that clear?'

Amil nodded.

'Good. First, you must check that your hands and the table are both clean and dry.'

Amil nodded again, wiping his hands on his shirt to show that he understood.

'Now, place one of those boxes on the end of the table. Remove the leaflets from it and stack them in neat piles by the side. When you have done that, move the empty box to the other end of the table, so that you may put the leaflets back into it when you have folded them.' When Amil had completed that task, Mr Kumar dragged a chair over to the table. 'Now, sit there and fold your first leaflet.'

Amil sat down. He took a sheet of paper from the nearest pile and folded it in half. Mr Kumar took the leaflet from him and held it up for inspection.

'You will have to do better than that,' he said. 'Look here, the corners are not perfectly aligned. And you have run your fingers too hard over the ink and smudged it. The leaflet is ruined. Try again, and this time be sure to align the corners perfectly.' He handed Amil a piece of rag. 'And wipe your face. Our customers do not want their leaflets covered in your sweat. Keep your back straight so that your head does not dangle over your work like a dripping tap. Am I making myself clear?'

Amil nodded. In doing so he dislodged a drop of sweat from the tip of his nose, which plopped on to the leaflet in front of him. Mr Kumar snatched it away and screwed it into a ball.

'These are simple instructions,' he said, throwing it across the room. 'Even a Gujar should be able to follow them. Now try again.'

Amil took another leaflet from the top of the pile. Mr Kumar loomed over him like a huge gravitational force, attracting mistakes. 'Remember, no smudges, no sweatmarks, no badly aligned corners – I do not wish to receive complaints about your shoddy workmanship.' Amil wiped his face with the cloth and blew gently on his fingers to ensure that they were dry. Then he folded the paper in half. Despite his hands shaking, and Mr Kumar peering over his shoulder, he aligned the corners perfectly. All he had to do now was smooth the crease down.

'Ouch!' A thin red line appeared on Amil's fingertip.

Mr Kumar clenched the tufts of hair protruding above his ears. 'Idiot! Paper can be as sharp as a blade, boy. Spread your fingers away from the edge, not along it. Do you think I can deliver leaflets to our customers that have your blood on them?'

'There is a water hand-pump in the street. Shall I go there to wash my finger?' Amil asked.

'And run away again? Do you take me for a fool?' Mr Kumar replied.

'I will not run away. I have promised my uncle Ravi.'

Mr Kumar hesitated for a moment. Then he waved his hand, and Amil ran out of the door. Amil had noticed that the hands on Mr Kumar's old watch never moved. Nevertheless, as he returned to the workshop barely a minute later, Mr Kumar made a point of tapping the glass with his fingernail. 'In business, time is money,' he said.

'I am sorry, Mr Kumar. I was as quick as possible.'

Mr Kumar pointed to the chair. 'Try again,' he said.

A few minutes later, Amil had successfully folded a handful of leaflets to Mr Kumar's satisfaction.

'At last,' said Mr Kumar. 'Now you will fold every leaflet, in every one of those boxes, by the end of today. Do you understand?' Amil nodded. 'And if I find a single one that has not been folded to the highest standard, you will be in for a beating, do you understand that, too?' Amil nodded again.

Mr Kumar swept out of the workshop, leaving the door open so that Amil could make the most of the day's light. And he needed every moment of it. Even working non-stop throughout the day, pausing only to rub his aching back or wash and dry his sticky hands, it was not until sunset that he packed the last few folded leaflets back into their box. Mr Kumar arrived shortly afterwards, swaying, it appeared to Amil, as though he were standing on a boat. He retrieved a few leaflets from each box then stepped outside to examine them under the lamplight, before dropping them back on to the table with a grunt of approval. Then he closed the door behind him, leaving it unlocked.

Amil leaned back in his chair. Even though he was slippery with sweat and his fingers felt as stiff as twigs, he was relieved to have survived his first day at work, and without a beating. He flexed his fingers as if he were playing an invisible piano, his silent symphony cut short a few seconds later by the clunk of the door hatch sliding shut behind him. He turned to find a small bowl of rice waiting for him on the floor, its rim once again decorated with small floury fingerprints. Realising that the attic had remained unlocked, Amil took the bowl upstairs. There, sitting cross-legged on the trunk under the fading light, he dipped his fingers into the warm rice and began spooning it into his mouth.

When he had finished, he set the bowl down and licked his fingers clean. Then he stood up on the trunk, pushing aside the sheet of plastic that covered the skylight so that he could gaze out. As the hot stale air in the attic rushed past him into the night like a heavy sigh of bad breath, he gulped back the slightly cooler, fresher air streaming in to take its place. Directly ahead of him, clearly visible beyond the sea of dilapidated shacks about which Mr Kumar complained so bitterly, the pesticide plant stood lit up like a space station, its steel chimneys and storage tanks rising like giant silver space rockets ready for launch. Even without his telegraph pole he could see the future, and knew still that one day he would be part of it. One day, like his uncle Ravi, he would wear a uniform and a helmet and set off to wage war against the bugs. His family were farmers now – there was no battle more worth fighting.

As he stepped down from the trunk, a bat, disturbed from its slumbers in the eaves, whooshed past him through the skylight. Amil stumbled, and as he slipped off the trunk, one of his sandals clipped the ancient padlock, snapping it off. From his pocket, Amil pulled out his new torch and inspected the damage. Fortunately, the lock looked as though it had simply rusted through with age.

Relieved that he could not be accused of forcing open the trunk, Amil decided to take a quick look inside.

The moment he lifted the lid he unleashed a smell that pushed his head back like a heavy punch. He put his hand over his mouth and nose, and poked around inside the trunk with the end of his torch. At first, there seemed little of interest. Most of the space was taken up with a large piece of thick canvas. He dragged it out and unrolled it, noting the strong brass eyelets in each corner and the four thick leather straps leading from them. Wrapped inside it he found a small canvas kitbag, waxy to the touch and held closed by a drawstring. Holding the kitbag at arm's length, he emptied it on to the floor. Among its contents were dozens of dead spiders, each one curled up into a ball as though it had stumbled into a sudden, agonising death-trap. Set in their midst, like a memorial in a spidery graveyard, was a plain grey pebble. A thin leather cord had been threaded through the hole in its centre, prompting Amil to place it over his head like a necklace. As he shone his torch back on to the floor, a pair of huge beady eyes stared up at him from the middle of a ghostly white face, devoid of nose or mouth. Amil cried out, before realising that they were not eyes at all, but round glass windows set into the side of a cloth sack. Once his heart had stopped pounding, he directed his light to examine it more closely. He had no idea why a sack would have windows set into the side of it, but through one of them he could see that the sack was not empty. Tentatively, he reached in and pulled out a battered brown leather journal. Its cover was plain except for the initials *SG*, stamped in gold leaf that had long ago lost its shine. He turned the book around in his hands. Then, with a quiet papery creak, he opened it.

The yellowed pages felt as brittle as dry leaves. Those in the second half of the journal were blank, as though whatever story the book told had been cut short, like a railway journey that had abruptly run out of track. But there was more than enough in the first half to attract Amil's attention. These pages were filled with faded blue handwriting, punctuated at regular intervals with scribbled drawings, often accompanied by short annotations. Some of the drawings he recognised as people, many of them lying down in strange, twisted shapes that left Amil feeling uneasy, as though he were being taken into yet another alien world. There were other odd things too, like a horse with huge, outstretched wings, and clouds with strange elongated words printed beneath them in a language that he did not recognise. And filling the margins, and every available space around the text, were swirls and spirals and geometric patterns which appeared not to be doodles, but were drawn with precision and purpose, as though they were mapping the trajectory of a spiralling vulture or a ricocheting bullet. None of the illustrations, Amil knew, would make proper sense until he read the story that accompanied them. But first he would need to make himself comfortable. He looked down at the large piece of canvas on the floor, then up at the two wooden support beams that ran across the width of the attic. A few minutes later, having once again used the trunk for extra height, he had rigged up a makeshift hammock. Cocooned in it, he hoped he would be safe from any rats or cockroaches that might scurry around the floor at night, and from any intruders in the workshop below which, he had noticed, Mr Kumar had failed to lock. Amil took off the pebble necklace and carefully returned everything he was not using to the trunk, before heaving it on to the hatch. Finally, feeling a little more secure, he climbed into the hammock, and shone his torch on to the first page of the journal.

'Today,' he read, 'I am jub . . . jub . . .'

'Jubilant!' The low, croaky voice had come from the pile of rags in the corner. 'And please be careful with my journal. It is old and fragile, like me.'

Amil leaped down from the hammock and ran to the trunk, pushing it off the hatch so that he could make his escape.

'There is no need to run,' the voice told him. Amil aimed his torch at the rag pile, and two milky-yellow eyes shone back at him. A skeletal hand emerged from the rags to shield them from the light. 'Would you mind pointing that contraption somewhere else, young man,' the voice asked quietly. 'I am not used to bright lights.' But Amil kept the beam fixed on the corner, his spare hand poised over the hatch, ready to pull it up.

'Who are you?' he demanded.

'I am a blind man, or at least I will be if you do not lower that light. Do not be afraid. Look at me . . . I am far too old to do you any harm.' Slowly, the man lowered his hand, and closed his eyes against the light. True to his word, he looked older than anyone Amil had ever seen. His head was threadbare, hairless but for a few delicate wisps that fell to his shoulders like strands of silver cotton. A handful more sprouted around his mouth and chin, framing a face that was pitted and criss-crossed with deep crevices, as though it had been mined for any trace of youth. Even under the glare of his torch, Amil found it hard to tell where the rags ended and the creases in the old man's face began.

'Who are you?' Amil asked again, lowering the beam.

The man looked up. 'I am your great-grandfather – your pardada, Sanjiv Gujar,' he said. 'I am the reason you are here.'

6

Marching Like Peacocks

Amil pinched himself. Surely the old man was just another character in his nightmare. He moved closer, glancing down at the journal that he had dropped into the hammock. The initials on the cover were clear enough. *SG.* Sanjiv Gujar.

'Mr Kumar says that you are a coward. And that you betrayed three of his ancestors and left them to die.'

The old man sighed. 'And you believe him?'

'No. But I believe my uncle Ravi, and my mother and father, and they all agree that there is a family debt which must be paid. And that it is because of you.'

'Perhaps they are all mistaken,' the old man replied. 'For do not stories change with every telling? Do they not get twisted and misshapen by the winds of time, like the branches of an old tree?'

'Perhaps,' said Amil.

'Then would you not rather know the true story of what happened all those years ago?'

Amil nodded. Now that he was confident he could

outrun the wizened old man, he climbed back into the hammock, and returned to the first page. 'Why is your writing so wobbly?' he asked. 'Were you shaking with fear?'

The old man made a raw throaty sound which Amil took to be a chuckle. 'No. I was not shaking with fear. I began writing the journal whilst on board a ship, ploughing a very uncomfortable furrow through stormy seas on my way to France. If you have ever tried to write a letter whilst riding on the back of a drunken elephant, you will understand. But my story does not begin on the ship, or even in France.'

'Where does it begin?' Amil asked. A spindly finger emerged slowly from the rags and pointed to the skylight.

'Out there,' said Sanjiv. 'Take a look.'

Amil jumped down from the hammock and dragged the trunk over to the skylight. He climbed up and peeled back the plastic sheeting.

'What do you see?' asked Sanjiv.

'I see thousands of shacks made from planks and pieces of corrugated iron,' Amil replied. 'Mr Kumar calls it a slum and says that the Gujars are to blame for him living amid such riff-raff and squalor. Beyond that is the pesticide plant where my uncle Ravi works. Its lights are covering everything in an orange glow.'

'How things have changed,' said Sanjiv. 'In nineteen-fourteen, were you to have looked out of that window as I

45

did, you would not have seen orange, but a sea of khaki brown. You would have seen the uniforms of a thousand Indian soldiers, as they marched in perfect unison across the parade ground on which those shacks now stand.'

Amil returned to the hammock, as the old man continued his story.

'I remember, many years earlier, seeing those soldiers for the first time. My family were farmers, as yours are now. One year their whole crop was wiped out by an infestation of great hairy caterpillars. My father was unable to feed us all, so he decided that as I was the oldest and strongest, he would bring me to Bhopal so that I might find my own way in the world. For a day we walked the streets together, asking every tradesman and street vendor whether I might become their apprentice in return for food and somewhere to sleep. But, even though the streets and alleyways were hot and sweaty with activity, we met no one who required the services of a nine-year-old farm boy, skilled only in the tilling of soil and the feeding of chickens.

'At the end of the day our wanderings took us to the old parade ground. There, the Bhopal Infantry – the "Bo-Peeps", as they were called – would practise their marching drills and, once a year, present themselves in all their finery for the inspection of the princess of Bhopal, as well as the Commander of the Indian Army, no less than the representative of the king of England himself. By the luck of the gods, it was on that very day that we found ourselves joining the citizens of Bhopal to witness this great display, as row upon row of our fine Indian warriors – their buttons and badges glinting like stars, their rifles slung proudly over their squared shoulders – marched like peacocks under the eyes of their British and Indian officers. The entire Kumar family had come out to watch this grand parade, including the four brothers who were to become my best friends. We stood next to them in the crowd. Our fathers talked together, despite the sound of marching feet and cheering onlookers. I did not hear what was said, but I remember Old Mr Kumar nodding, and my father shaking him by the hand. Then I felt my father hug me, even though my eyes remained fixed on the grand spectacle unfolding in front of me. When, finally, the parade ended and I looked round, he was gone. That was the last time I saw him, or any of my family.'

'Why did you not see them again?' asked Amil.

'Because they were eaten by a great hairy caterpillar,' Sanjiv replied.

Amil's eyes widened. 'Really?'

The rags stirred as Sanjiv slowly shook his head. 'No. But they might just as well have been. Old Mr Kumar told me that the year after the caterpillars came there was a drought, so that nothing grew at all. And the year after that, the caterpillars returned to eat my family's crop all over again. They did not survive.'

For a moment, Amil thought of his own family, and wondered whether caterpillars would eat their crops too. He turned the page, and Sanjiv continued.

'After the parade, Old Mr Kumar introduced me to his wife and his four sons. The youngest of them was Mani, who was still in his mother's arms. Then came Deepak and Dev, who were a couple of years younger than me. They were born nine months apart, but looked and behaved as if it were no more than nine minutes. Both were small and wiry, and so full of energy that they bounced around the streets of Bhopal like fireworks in a bucket. Every day, Old Mr Kumar gave them messages to deliver around the city, sometimes entirely unnecessary ones, hoping that by the time they took their places in the family printing business their reckless energy would have dissipated. But it never did. Instead, they sought out adventure and mischief wherever they could find it, the only real difference between them being that whilst Deepak could talk the hind legs off a donkey, Dev would be more likely to leap on to its back and ride off with it. Either way, both of them would end up being chased by its owner. When they were older, and clever words and innocent smiles were not enough to get them out of trouble, they developed another skill. Running. Very few people could catch them, and on the rare occasions when they did, their big brother Kush, with his broad shoulders and quick, powerful hands, would usually turn up to rescue them from the local ruffians.

'Kush was nine, like me, but he was bigger and stronger. I was to take over some of his more menial duties in the family business so that he could attend school. That was the deal struck between our two fathers. With Deepak and Dev off together running into trouble and Mani yet to escape his mother's grip, Kush and I soon became the best of friends. He would complain that it was my fault that he had to attend school, when he would rather be working in the business with his father. But he knew that the son of a printer – let alone one that published fine works of literature – had to be educated. Even though the Kumar family is of a higher caste than ours, Amil, Kush took me under his wing. He taught me everything he learned in school, including how to read and write, and stood up for me whenever anyone tried to poke fun at the scrawny country boy. Whenever he was not at school he would share my work, and we made numerous excursions together around the city, pulling the handcart that you have just oiled, collecting supplies of ink and paper, and delivering books of poetry to customers the length and breadth of Bhopal.

'In time, Kush returned to the business and it was the turn of Deepak and Dev to go to school, to the great relief of Old Mr Kumar. In the years that followed, Kumar and Sons prospered, even though Deepak and Dev were like coiled springs in the workshop, seeking any opportunity to leave their posts minding the machines to run errands around the city. At the same time Kush and I read every book of poetry his father printed. These were not poems about everyday life. They transported us to the realms of gods, where epic battles raged between good and evil, and the air was filled with honour and sacrifice and the roaring cut and thrust of heroic deeds. Often, we would wish to be inside the world that these poems imagined, to live the words rather than merely read them. For how could a life spent reading of honour and glory match even a single day spent as a real warrior?

Every week, as the Bhopal Infantry marched up and down the parade ground next door, we would find ourselves printing and cutting and folding and packing to the sound of their pounding feet, each taunting crunch of their boots reminding us of the world of glory and adventure that lay outside. Though it was never said, the four of us (for Mani was still very young) yearned for a life beyond the workshop. And Old Mr Kumar knew it. As soon as their sons were old enough, he and his wife began looking for suitable wives who might bear them children, knowing that the duties of fatherhood would dampen their appetite for adventure. But arrangements had yet to be made. In the meantime, it was I who took a wife, knowing that as the sole survivor of my family I had a duty to continue the Gujar name.'

'Was she pretty?' Amil asked.

Sanjiv nodded slowly. 'She was beautiful,' he said. 'Her name was Naisha. We married in nineteen-fourteen, shortly before the emperor, the king of England, declared war on his great foe the German kaiser. That year the Grand Parade was different from other years. The Bo-Peeps were about to depart for France to fight alongside the British, and as the Kumar brothers and I watched them parade that day, we no longer saw peacocks marching. We saw lions. For it was not the sunlight glinting on their buttons that stirred us, but the steely glint in their eyes and the purpose in their stride.

When we returned to the workshop afterwards, Kush announced to his father that he and his brothers wished to volunteer for the army. Old Mr Kumar quietly led the three of them outside and pointed to the fine lettering inscribed above the workshop doors. "Look," he told them, "the sign clearly says *Kumar and Sons*. And *Sons*. This is where you belong, not on some far-flung battlefield." They knew better than to argue with their father so, silently, they returned to the workshop. But, whilst they continued to honour their father's wishes, it was clear to everyone, including a succession of prospective wives and their parents, that they were far from "settled". There was a pacing, fidgeting restlessness to them that no amount of hard work could assuage. Old Mr and Mrs Kumar refused to see it, or even acknowledge the war. But, one day, several months later, everything changed.

'On that day, we had all been working hard to print a very special book of poetry. Bound in the finest silver thread, it had been commissioned by the princess. Although we had always delivered books to the palace, today it was to be Old Mr Kumar's great honour to present this book to the princess in person. On her return from inspecting a new contingent of volunteers, the princess's carriage came to a halt outside the workshop. Framed by our open doorway in a pool of sunlight, its horses and riders motionless, it appeared for a moment as though Old Mr Kumar was stepping from the workshop into a painting. As he approached the carriage, the princess held out her hand to him. In it, with a slight bow, he placed the first pristine copy of the new book which we had printed for her. She spoke a few words to him, and then the carriage was gone.

'It should have been a joyous occasion for Old Mr Kumar, and I expected him to turn to us, flushed with pride. Instead, he remained in the street, still and silent, as if the princess had turned him to stone.

'As we all ate together that night, after much poking

and prodding from his wife, Old Mr Kumar revealed what the princess had said to him.

' "She told me that her son had gone to help the emperor defeat the German kaiser . . ."

' "What else did she say?" Old Mrs Kumar asked.

' "She asked me whether our sons had any plans to do the same."

'I remember Old Mrs Kumar's eyes growing wide and fearful. "I hope you told her that we do not consider this to be India's war."

'Old Mr Kumar hesitated, and our mouths ceased chewing. "How could I?" he said solemnly. "I informed her that our sons would do their duty."

'As Old Mrs Kumar stifled a shriek, Kush and his brothers leaped up . . .'

'. . . jubilant?' Amil continued.

'That is right,' said Sanjiv. 'Jubilant. For, at last, they were to become warriors.'

7

Arrival in France

'Welcome back.' The low, croaky voice had come from the pile of rags in the corner of the room. Amil rubbed his eyes and stretched. 'You fell asleep, although I cannot blame you. Folding paper can be very tiring. And dull too. Perhaps you can understand why Kush and his brothers were so keen to go on an adventure.'

Amil picked up the journal. The old man nestled back into the rag pile, his eyes like slits, fixed on the rusty corrugated roof above him.

'Shall we continue?'

Amil yawned, nodding.

'Early the next day, Kush and his two brothers went to the recruiting depot, much to the annoyance of Mani, who was not old enough to go too. I went with them, keeping them company as they joined a long queue which stretched outside the building. Whilst some may have been there out of a sense of duty to the British Empire and others, like Kush and his brothers, to quench their thirst for the warrior life, most were straggly, barefooted fellows who looked as though they could hardly lift a rifle, let alone carry one into battle. They were farmers mostly, half-starved after another long drought, desperate for a decent meal and a regular pay packet to send home to their families in the country. I had not planned to sign up. I had just taken a wife, and even though I yearned to fight side by side with Kush and his brothers, I knew where my duty lay. But then a whisper spread down the queue, promising that there would be a great reward for our loyalty to the emperor. Freedom from British rule. At that moment, I could think of no greater gift to bestow on my wife, and the sons and daughters that one day she would bear me. So, I signed my name too.

'When I returned home Naisha knew what I had done the moment I walked through the door. She said I looked three inches taller. Tears welled up in her eyes and she clutched her belly. But I could see that she was not clutching it in fear. She was cradling it. Then she looked up at me and smiled, and my heart leaped as she told me that, by the time I returned home, I would be a father.'

Sanjiv let out a deep sigh.

'So . . . that is how the Kumar brothers and I came to be on that ship. How is my handwriting now?'

'Much better,' replied Amil. 'It is not so wobbly.'

'Ah! That is because our ship has finally arrived in France. At a place called Marseille. From there, we caught a train north, rattling through open farmland which looked rich and plentiful, beyond the dreams of most of the farmers on board. As the train whistled through the village stations along our route, crowds lining the platforms cheered us on like heroes. Our spirits began to soar as we contemplated the glorious and noble endeavour in which we were about to take part. Finally, our train journey ended at a station on the outskirts of a small town.

'Like the countryside through which we had passed, the town seemed untouched by the fighting, with barely a tile out of place on its buildings. Cheered on by the local people, we marched through the town square, continuing on until the shops gave way to houses which, in turn, gave way to the scattering of farms and outbuildings in which we were to be based. Two Indian soldiers were there to meet us, and took us to a barn that would serve as our sleeping quarters for the next few days. On the way I remarked to one of them that, despite the cloudless sky, we had better prepare for a rainstorm, given the rumble of thunder I could hear in the distance. He turned to his partner, shaking his head, then back at me. But he did not reply. Instead, he seemed to stare through me, as though I was not by his side but a thousand miles away, across a gulf too wide for him to breach with idle conversation.

'I turned to Kush and shrugged. "Did I say something wrong?"

'He looked at the soldier, then back at me. "I think

what you are hearing is the noise of battle, Sanjiv. There is no need to put up your umbrella just yet."

'I felt foolish, I can tell you. I realised that, for the soldier, the gulf between us was as wide as an ocean, one that could be crossed only when I had seen what he had seen, heard what he had heard, and felt what he had felt. To him I was only half-formed, almost invisible.

'That night our British company commander came to meet us. His name was Captain Bradbury. Kush and I were standing outside the barn door when he arrived on his horse, to be greeted by the two soldiers who had escorted us there.'

'What colour was his horse?' Amil asked.

'She was a white mare,' replied Sanjiv. 'A very fine beast, called Bo. He had brought her with him all the way from Bhopal, hoisted on and offboard ship in the horse sling that you are using for a hammock. Perhaps you can smell her, even now.'

Amil turned his head and sniffed the canvas. It did not smell of horse. Rather, it smelled of something sharp that pricked the back of his throat and made him cough.

He shook his head, and Sanjiv continued. 'He passed the reins of his horse to the farmer's daughter, who had emerged from the farmhouse. Then he watched her as she led it to a water trough set under the shade of a nearby tree. Only when it was safely tethered and quenching its thirst did he cross the courtyard towards us. He was smaller than the two men walking either side of him, so that he appeared to be under their protection. But stories of his prowess in battle had already reached us, so we knew that not to be the case. We knew already that he was always first into the fight, and rightly so. But he had a reputation for toughness that went beyond bravery. In the short walk between the farmhouse and the barn I noticed that even his face and hands, the only two parts of him not concealed by his uniform, appeared strong and angular, as though they had been carved with a broad chisel, in a material too hard to smooth off. Only his round glasses and the wisps of curly red hair protruding from the side of his cap softened his otherwise square-cut demeanour.

'Inside the barn, he announced that we would be joining the rest of his company once we had been issued with warm clothing and new rifles, and spent a few days on a nearby artillery range learning to fire them. Then, he moved informally among us, talking to one group after another. Most of the new recruits were farmers who had decided that they would rather get paid to fight the Germans on a full stomach, than stay at home to fight swarms of locusts on an empty one. He spoke to each of them in turn, discussing crops and the pests that plagued them in a way that only a fellow farmer, or at least the son of one, could. I overheard one of the farmers, a skinny fellow whose bones looked sharp enough to puncture his skin, tell him that it was probably easier to crack a German helmet than the hide of a rhinoceros beetle. Captain Bradbury told him that we would all find out soon enough, and the two soldiers with him glanced at each other, as if already they knew the answer.

'Then he came to talk to us. When we said that we were not farmers but from the city, he told us that he had been with the Bhopal Infantry for five years, and that to him the city felt like home. He told us that he was from a place called Oxford in England. The lakes in Bhopal reminded him of the river which ran through it, he told us, and the great golden domes of its mosques and temples stood as fine as Oxford's ancient spires. When Kush told him that the Kumar family business printed books of poetry, he was even more delighted. Like Bhopal, he said, the streets of his home city hummed with literature and culture. That is why the two cities felt to him like twins, ruled over by the same king. So, how could he feel homesick? He said all of this in Hindi, which impressed every man in the barn that night. At the end of the evening, having learned of Deepak and Dev's running prowess, he assigned them to be his new runners. Their job would be to carry messages between fighting units and beyond. To Kush and me, he gave the responsibility of transcribing letters home for the many country soldiers who could not write, a task which we began that night under the light of an oil lamp. As he left, the two soldiers stiffened to attention before escorting him outside. There they remained, watchful, until he had disappeared into the warm glow of the farmhouse opposite.

'In the morning the farmer's daughter reached in through the barn door to deliver us two buckets of water with which to wash ourselves. Throughout the week the face of the girl remained a mystery, permanently shrouded from view by her long black hair as she spent the day stooped over a broom or a shovel, or scattering feed for the chickens which roamed the courtyard.

'On that first day, we marched to our company headquarters situated in an old manor house on the other side of the town. There we received our new rifles. We were also each handed a small canvas bag containing something which looked like a white sack, inset with two windows, like the portholes of a ship.'

'I found one like it in the trunk,' Amil said. 'What is it?'

'I asked Kush the same question as we were leaving,' Sanjiv replied. ' "Clearly, it is to protect us from the smoke of battle," he explained to me, "like a protective mask." He pulled it over his head like a hood and tucked the bottom under the collar of his uniform. Then he stared at me through its huge round eyes.

' "You look like a ghost," I told him. "You will not need

a bayonet to kill the enemy. You will frighten them to death."

'Our light-hearted mood continued throughout the week as we marched to and from the practice range. Those escorting us had been there over the winter, and kept warning us about the cold and the mud and the perils of neglecting to keep one's feet dry. But the worst of the weather appeared to be over, with nothing but a few cotton wool clouds in the sky. Once our final day of training was over, the kit we were given to take to the front seemed unnecessary. Thick and itchy, our new uniforms and heavy coats felt as weighty as the ammunition each of us carried.

'When we arrived in the town square, Captain Bradbury and the remains of his company, which we were to reinforce, had already assembled. As we joined them, I noticed that these men were not like the soldiers I had seen marching on the parade ground in Bhopal. They appeared to have lost all pride in their appearance. There were several jokers among them, too.

'"What fine glinting buttons, you have," one said to me. "The enemy snipers will be grateful to you for lighting up their target."

'"And what finely polished boots," said another. "It is a pity that soon you will be up to your knees in mud."

'The frivolity continued as we marched out of the square. But as the rumble of thunder grew louder, and the flashes of lightning grew brighter against the evening sky, so the soldiers fell to silence and their mood darkened. Kush and I, with Deepak and Dev behind us, marched towards it wrapped in our own thoughts, oblivious to everything except the back of the preceding man, as though seeking comfort amid the soft, undulating folds of his uniform. Soon, even thoughts did not intrude on us, as the rhythmic *crunch, crunch, crunch, crunch* of marching feet sent us into a walking sleep.'

8

At War Against the Bugs

Buzz, buzzz, *buzzzz*. The tickly fly on Amil's lip buzzed like an alarm clock, growing louder and more insistent as he stirred awake. Eventually, he batted it away and sat up in the hammock, feeling as hot and sticky as the air pressing round him. The journal had fallen from his grasp as he slept. It lay closed on the floor. He jumped down and returned it carefully to the trunk.

'Pardada? *Pardada!*'

There was no response from the pile of rags in the corner. He rubbed his eyes. They stung, like his throat. He heard the hatch slide shut in the workshop and raced down to eat the paratha that had been pushed through for him. As usual the plate bore Chunni's floury trademark. He had spent little time with Chunni since his arrival at the Kumars', but today they were to make a trip together through the Old City of Bhopal. More than one, he guessed, because clearly the leaflets he had folded the previous day could not be delivered in a single journey. Despite devouring all his breakfast his stomach still felt hollow, as though trepidation had instantly gnawed away every morsel. For even though her floury fingerprints had already become a welcome sight, Chunni had not yet smiled at him. He did not know what the day would bring. If she was anything like her brother and father, she might think nothing of beating him if he did something wrong, and he was in no position to fight back. He heard light footsteps approaching. The door swung open.

'Are you ready?' Chunni asked. Amil licked his fingers clean and placed the plate on the trestle table as Chunni wheeled the cart over to the boxes. 'The wheels no longer squeak,' she observed, matter-of-factly.

Amil took this to be a compliment. 'Thank you,' he replied.

They began to load up the cart. Twelve boxes, four per load. They would need to make three trips. Amil could not keep up with Chunni, who loaded three boxes in the time it took him to load one.

'I am used to lifting heavy things,' she told him. 'I could carry you over my shoulder like a sack of rice if I wanted to.' She picked up the handle of the cart. It was T-shaped at the end so that it could be pulled with two hands, or by two people walking side by side. 'I will take it first,' Chunni said. 'You close the door behind us.'

Even under a full load, Amil's maintenance work passed

inspection. The wheels remained mute. They walked up the street in silence, away from the slums and towards the shops, mosques and ancient temples of the Old City. There, every building was festooned with strings of Diwali lanterns and fragrant garlands of golden marigolds, ready for the Festival of Lights celebrations that were to take place that night. Chunni stared straight ahead, seemingly unmoved by the lavish decorations around them. But, for Amil, they were a bittersweet reminder of the Diwalis he used to spend with his family. Every year, under the watchful eye of their father, he and his brothers would light candles in their windows to invite Lakshmi, the Goddess of Wealth, into their home, before exchanging gifts and tucking into their grandmother's delicious homemade sweets. And when every morsel had been eaten, and every finger licked clean, he and his brothers, his mother and father and his grandparents, would set off together to watch the fireworks that celebrated the triumph of good over evil. For a few moments, he tried to immerse himself in these happy memories, only to find that they made him miss his family even more. Finally, he turned to Chunni.

'Will you go with your father to the celebrations tonight?' he asked her.

'No,' she said. 'He says that, thanks to your family, we have nothing to celebrate, and that clearly the gods deserted us many years ago, especially Lakshmi. Jalesh and his friends will go to a fireworks display and run around like idiots setting off firecrackers. But I must stay indoors and clean the house.' She continued walking, her strides long and purposeful. Amil found it hard to keep pace with her in his new sandals, stumbling whenever he was distracted by the rich aromas of street food and flower stalls, or the honking of a car horn. Each time, the front of the cart would catch up with him and clip his heels, causing him to yelp with pain. Occasionally, Chunni would turn her head to acknowledge the greeting of a street vendor or passerby. But she showed no interest in talking to Amil.

'When I was looking for oil for the wheels I found some paint and brushes,' he said, eventually. 'Shall I paint the cart so that *Kumar and Sons* may be read more clearly?'

Chunni's eyes remained fixed ahead. 'Not unless you want a beating from my father,' she replied. 'He says that Kumar and Sons is over one hundred years old, and that the faded lettering reflects our seniority. He says that he does not wish us to be mistaken for some fly-by-night business still wet behind the ears. So he refuses to change it.' She continued walking, turning towards a part of Bhopal that Amil had not visited before.

'Where are we going?' he asked.

'We are taking these boxes to Mr Panwar,' Chunni

replied. 'He is the man who bought the printing press from my father.'

A few minutes later, having left the busy streets and alleyways of the Old City behind them, Amil found himself walking up a wide street, lined on either side with flat-roofed single storey buildings. Chunni headed for the nearest and dragged the cart through an open doorway in its side. Amil followed her. The room was similar in size to Kumar and Sons' workshop, however the clattering machines and people which filled it made it appear much smaller. Perhaps, thought Amil, this was what Kumar and Sons looked like when his father worked there.

Chunni called to a tall thin man bent over a machine at the far end of the workshop.

'Good morning, Mr Panwar!' As the man looked up, Chunni put her hands together in greeting. Amil followed suit. Mr Panwar tucked the oily rag he had been holding into the pocket of his brown ink-stained overalls and walked towards them, pausing only to exchange a word or two with the men operating the machines.

'Right on time, Chunni!' he said. He took the handle of the cart from her and rested it carefully against the wall, before lifting out the boxes and placing them side by side on a nearby workbench. Then he opened each one to examine a handful of the leaflets inside. 'Are they all done?' he asked her, his voice raised almost to a shout above the cacophony of the machines.

'Yes,' she replied, 'I will bring the other two loads later today. This is Amil. He is our new paper-folder. My father told me to tell you that we have "doubled our capacity."'

The man peered at Amil over the top of his reading glasses.

'The boy should be at school. And so should you.'

Chunni was keen to change the subject. 'Do you still have our printing press?' she asked.

'Of course I still have it. Who else will buy it from me except a museum?' The man led Chunni and Amil to a storeroom at the back of the workshop, separated from the main area by long strips of thick, clear plastic which hung from the top of a wide opening. The room was stacked with tins of coloured printing inks, alongside huge stacks of paper, piled high on pallets that only a forklift truck could carry. Behind them, pushed up against the whitewashed brickwork under an oil-stained blanket, sat the old printing press. Chunni peeled back its oily shroud.

'It is over one hundred years old,' she explained to Amil. 'My father sold it to Mr Panwar many years ago, but he has much better printing machines now. One day I will buy it back from him, and then I will print everything in colour.'

'Colour, indeed! Do not let your father hear you say

that,' Mr Panwar joked. 'You should have heard him the last time he was here. He saw us printing some colour leaflets for the pesticide plant. Each picture showed a different-coloured pest devouring a different-coloured crop. It was very educational. But your father was not impressed.

'"Save all that colour for decorating buses and saris," he told me. "If something is worth reading, it is worth reading in black and white – there is no need to dress it up like a damn peacock."'

Chunni dropped the blanket back over the press.

'Do you have anything for me to take away?' she asked. Mr Panwar took the rag from his pocket and inspected it.

'I think this one is past its best,' he said, lobbing it towards her.

She plucked it out of the air.

'Is that all?' she asked. The man smiled.

'Of course not, Chunni. There are two bag loads over there. We get through them like wildfire when we are busy.'

Chunni lifted one of the bags into the cart, and Amil the other. He noticed that the rags inside were similar to those in the attic, if considerably less crusty. 'Get what you can for them, Chunni. The quicker you can buy that old relic from me, the better. I will need the extra space soon.'

'For what?' Chunni asked.

Mr Panwar hesitated. He looked down at his feet. 'I have decided to buy a paper-folding machine,' he said.

The cart was much lighter on the return journey. Again, Amil offered to pull it along. Again, Chunni refused his help. A mile or so from the workshop, she cut down a side alley. At the end of it stood a large shack made from sheets of corrugated iron, each a different shade of rust from the next. Whilst a handful of them were bolted into position, the majority appeared to be tied together with little more than strips of cloth, threaded through convenient rust holes. As instructed, Amil waited by the door whilst Chunni wheeled the cart inside. She emerged a few minutes later, tucking a handful of rupees into the pocket of her dress. The cart was empty.

'You can take it now,' she said, holding the handle up to him.

Two more trips followed. On the second return journey the cart carried bags full of paper offcuts – thin strips cropped from the edges of a thousand printed leaflets. On the third, it carried empty ink cans. Each time their return journey took a different route, as Chunni called in at various recycling stations to obtain the best prices for her waste pickings, and drop a few more rupees into her pocket. They arrived back at Chunni's house to find Mr Kumar waiting for them. He tapped his watch.

'Three trips, Chunni, and it has taken you all day! The boy is supposed to help you, not turn you into a tortoise.' He grabbed Chunni's arm and pulled her towards the door. Amil wanted to tell him that they had also been busy collecting rags and wastepaper. But for some reason Chunni did not mention their various detours, so he thought better of it. She looked across at him, grateful for his silence, and he knew that now they shared a secret. Her father ushered her indoors to prepare their evening meal, pausing only to order Amil into the workshop. So he took the cart inside and closed the door. Exhausted, he curled up in it and fell asleep. Chunni woke him an hour later.

'There is a roti for you on the table,' she said quietly.

Amil rubbed his eyes and sat up. 'Why did you not tell your father where we had been? Would he not be pleased that you were working so hard?'

Chunni shook her head. 'I cannot tell him. I need all the extra money I can earn for food, and so that I can buy the printing press back from Mr Panwar. If my father takes it he will spend it in the tea house and we will have nothing to eat. Besides, he would be ashamed to admit that I was picking rags to put food in his stomach, or that we cannot really afford to eat meat. So, we pretend that the paper-folding business earns enough to support us, and he gives me ten rupees every Friday to buy a chicken, just to keep up appearances. He will even cross the road to avoid me if he sees that I have rags in the cart. That is also why I keep it tucked behind the sink. That way, if the cart is loaded with rags he can pretend not to see them. His pride is like a big sack over his head. And I cannot pull it off.'

Mr Kumar's voice rang out from the house. 'Chunni, where are you?' Chunni ran to the door just as Uncle Ravi opened it. He held it open for her and she ducked under his arm without breaking step. Amil's uncle watched her run into the house.

'Do you think she will tell her father that I am here? I am not supposed to visit more than once a week.'

Amil shook his head. 'I do not think so, Chachaji.'

'That is good,' his uncle replied. He looked at the small flatbread which Chunni had left for Amil.

'That is barely enough to feed a mouse,' he observed. 'And not a very hungry mouse, either. No wonder your arms are like pipe cleaners. I will try to bring food for you whenever I can. Today, I have brought you some ladoo for Diwali. Your auntie Maya made them especially for you.' He laid a small cloth on the floor and placed a jasmine-scented candle in its centre. This he surrounded with a dozen bitesize balls of orange sweetness. As Amil sat down opposite him he lit the candle.

'Happy Diwali, Amil.'

'Happy Diwali,' Amil replied. 'Please thank Chachiji for the ladoo. It is very kind of her.'

After gulping down his roti, Amil began slowly to eat his way through the sweets. Every few seconds, he would close his eyes to savour the rich floral aroma of the candle and the familiar, comforting smell of his Uncle Ravi, both competing for the attention of his nostrils.

The most remarkable thing about Uncle Ravi was that despite toiling day after day in the blazing sun, and despite the scents of spices, and baking flatbreads, and sweaty feet, and the excretions of animals of every description, all of which suffused the Bhopal air like a pungent invisible fog, he always smelled as though he had just emerged from a long luxurious bath.

'You always smell so clean, Chachaji,' said Amil, licking orange crumbs from his fingers.

'That is because, all day, every day, I work with soap,' his uncle explained. 'I have a very important job, which is to spread a soapy liquid over every joint and valve in the pesticide plant, and look for bubbles where poisonous gases might be escaping. Then someone else, who has an equally important job, tightens every suspect nut and bolt to make sure the leaks, however minuscule, are sealed. And if that does not work, someone who has an equally important job will replace the whole valve. Rest assured, there will be no leaks at the plant whilst my fellow soldiers and I are on watch.'

'You are soldiers?' Amil asked.

'Of course we are soldiers!' replied his uncle. He put on his plastic safety helmet and jumped to attention. 'Why else do you think I wear a uniform and a helmet? Make no mistake, we are at war –' he dropped to his knees and began playfully to prod Amil as though he were a potato leaf under attack – 'against miniature armies of creeping spider mites, and great buzzing clouds of potato moths, and weevils and beetles and every kind of bug-eyed monster that it is possible to imagine – armed with an array of weapons that only nature could devise to destroy our crops and starve us all to death. But we will defeat them, Amil. We will be victorious!'

He continued to poke Amil in the ribs mercilessly. Amil fought back, half-laughing, half-crying, until a wild flailing punch landed on his uncle's nose, and he fell back as though he had been shot. Then the two of them sat side by side in silence, catching their breath and nibbling the last of the sweets.

'Do you have officers who give you orders?' Amil asked after a while.

Uncle Ravi nodded. 'Of course. We have a safety officer, and an engineering officer, and a finance officer. We even have a general – our general manager – a fine commanding fellow who plans our strategies and tactics. He and the other officers give us our orders and we carry them out like the brave, obedient soldiers that we are.'

Gently, he squeezed Amil's hand. 'And you must be brave too, Amil. You must follow Mr Kumar's orders, so that one day our family debt will be paid and the Gujar name will be free of shame.' As the candle flickered out he stood up to leave. 'One more thing. No matter how much Mr Kumar deserves it, you must never punch *him* on the nose.'

9

Poison Tentacles

After his uncle left, Amil climbed into the attic and stood on the trunk. Through the skylight he watched the numerous Diwali fireworks displays as they lit up the dark, moonless sky over Bhopal. As the nearest reached its climax in a series of dazzling, multicoloured explosions, he pressed his hands tightly together and prayed to Lakshmi. He prayed not only for the prosperity of his family in the country, but also for the one million rupees with which, Mr Kumar had said, he could buy his freedom. He knew that Mr Kumar had made the promise in jest and that, anyway, he was unlikely to find the trunk suddenly brimming with money. Even so, when the fireworks ended, he checked inside it. When he saw that nothing had changed, he pulled a rather warm and misshapen Diwali sweet from his pocket and placed it in front of the rag pile.

'Pardadaji, I saved some ladoo for you.'

The rags did not stir, so Amil returned to the trunk and retrieved the journal. For a while he did not open it. Instead, he lay in the hammock staring up at the ceiling, thinking about Chunni, and how they shared a secret. Two, perhaps, if she had not told Mr Kumar about his visitor. He sniffed the air, noting that it no longer smelled of jasmine and his uncle. There was another smell. Something stronger even than the cloying odour of glue and white spirit that normally filled the attic, making his head swim. He opened the journal, and sniffed the pages. At the same time the rags stirred, drawing his attention back to the corner of the room. Amil saw that the sweet was gone, and the tip of Sanjiv's head began slowly to rise out of the rags, like the head of an ancient tortoise peeping timidly from its shell.

'I am glad those fireworks are over,' said Sanjiv. 'They remind me too much of war.'

Amil's nostrils flared as the old man stretched a bare foot out from beneath the rags, and rested it on the floor for his inspection.

'Trench foot,' he explained. 'There is more life between my toes than in a well-stocked zoo. That is what happens if you stand in the mud for long enough. You begin to rot from the ground up.' Amil pinched his nose, and Sanjiv drew his bony leg back into the rag pile. 'That is where we lived you see, in a trench, dug deep into the ground like a furrow cut by a giant plough. For hundreds of miles it stretched, with other trenches running parallel behind it, and yet more connecting them all together, like a huge, elongated maze. Below them were our dug-outs – deep

77

underground chambers in which we might rest and shelter when our duties permitted it. When we arrived our trench was dry, the ground firm under foot. I did not understand why the soldiers who had escorted us there were not finely turned out; why their boots were not polished. I found out soon enough. The thunder and lightning I had heard on my arrival may indeed have been the sound of battle, stilled for the time being, but the rain did come. And with no trees or crops or even weeds left in the fields to soak it up, the bare earth quickly turned to mud. Soon it lay thick and black in the bottom of our trench, with us oozing around in it like maggots in an open wound.

'We stood knee-deep in it for weeks on end, awaiting our first encounter with the enemy. They were just a few hundred yards away, similarly entombed in their own trenches with little but the sky to look at. Occasionally, there would be a single shot as snipers from either side fired at any fellow foolish enough to poke his head above the trench wall. Kush was shot at several times, so keen was he to eye up the enemy. I had never seen a man so itching for battle.' The old man chuckled. 'I was just itching. Or at least my feet were. And my head, of course. Lice love soldiers almost as much as they love children.'

Instinctively, Amil scratched his scalp. 'What did you do all day?' he asked.

'More than most, fortunately,' Sanjiv replied. 'Captain

Bradbury kept Deepak and Dev busy. They were used to running through the streets, not wading knee-high through a swamp, so every message along the trench took them twice as long to deliver. But Kush and I were glad. Standing around waiting for battle to begin would have driven both of them mad.'

Sanjiv paused for a moment, tipping back his head to sniff the air, cautiously. Then he continued: 'Kush and I were lucky too. As the captain had put us in charge of writing letters home for the other men, he would invite us every day into his dug-out to discuss their morale. When we told him that the men were complaining to their loved ones about the cold, he ordered additional braziers for the trench, and extra rations of tea so that they may also warm their spirits. If we told him that they were complaining about being hungry, he would send Deepak and Dev squelching through the mud to our company headquarters to request more food. His men came first, except, according to those who had been into battle with him, when it was time to advance. Then he led from the front as we all expected. Although most of us were new recruits and had not yet fought with him, he made us feel safe, like a father, even though he was just a few years older than us. Because his family were farmers, he would talk to the soldiers about their crops, and the pests that had arrived to plague them. And, of course, like any farmer, and any Englishman, he would talk about the weather. Although Kush and I were not farmers, Captain Bradbury's love of poetry made us feel at ease in his company. He kept a few small books of poetry on a shelf in his dug-out, some of which had been written by his fellow officers. On one occasion, he took one from the shelf and lay in Bo's sling, which he had strung up as a hammock, much as you have done, and began to read it to us. He translated the poems as best he could, but we were sure that he must have made some errors in their translation. For they described war as a kind of hell, full only of death and destruction and despair. They conveyed nothing of the heroism and honour of the battlefield, as we had been expecting. We found them most unsettling. When we asked him why these poems did not celebrate the glory of battle, the captain snapped the book shut.

'"You will see," he said.

'But we did not see. The poems described a war that we did not recognise and could not imagine. When Captain Bradbury saw the look of bemusement on our faces, he reached quickly for another book. This one I found much more to my liking. It was called the *International Cloud Atlas*, and was full of pictures of clouds with strange names.'

Amil turned a page of the journal. 'There are pictures of clouds in here, too,' he said.

'That is because the clouds in the captain's book had such unusual shapes that I had to copy them down. Would you believe that there is a cloud called a mammatus that looks like the udder of a cow? I told the farmers this and they laughed at me. They said that if it were true, surely such a cloud would rain milk. But it is true. Just as it is true that there are clouds that look like castles in the air, or that stretch across the sky like the silvery trails of giant slugs. Who would not want to record such wonders?'

'Why did the captain have a book about clouds?' asked Amil.

'Because one day he wished to fly among them,' replied Sanjiv.

'Like a bird?' said Amil.

His great-grandfather chuckled, which led to a fit of coughing that left him gasping for breath.

'Like . . . the pilot . . . of an aeroplane, you nincompoop! His brother was a pilot. Captain Bradbury told me once that his deepest wish was for his white mare to sprout wings, so that he could fly into battle alongside his brother. He always had his ears pricked for the sound of an engine. Whenever a British aeroplane buzzed over our trench, the captain would rush from his dug-out to wave his helmet in the air, just in case his brother happened to be in the cockpit. One day, a few weeks before we arrived, he waved it too high. The bullet of a sniper pinged straight through it. When first Kush and I noticed the hole in his helmet, we were informed by the other soldiers that

Captain Bradbury had been shot in the head, but that on reaching his forehead the bullet had stopped instantly, and fallen to the ground like a dead fly. I knew then that they would continue to mock us until we had been into battle with them. Kush knew that too, and he was looking forward to the day when he could prove himself. After almost a month in the trench, that day arrived.

'Kush and I had left our dug-out just after sunrise. The night had been uneventful, and another day of boredom and frustration appeared to have begun. As we headed for the warmth of the brazier, there was a whistle, and a thud, and a lookout fell back into our path. The periscope through which he had been spying on the enemy had been cut clean in half. As Kush and I pulled him out of the mud, I recognised the soldier as one of those who had escorted us from the town.

'"That is like the first drop of the monsoon rains," he said, turning hastily towards the dug-out. "You can put up that umbrella now!"

'Kush grabbed my shoulder. "Come on, we must get underground." As we turned another shell fell, then another, bringing clods of earth raining down on us, and sounds I had not expected to hear, hisses and pings, as unseen assassins filled the air, seeking to strip the flesh from our bones like swarms of razor-toothed locusts. As fast as we could we sloshed through the mud, our heads bowed as if in homage to the forces being unleashed upon us. Then, as we reached the entrance the sky stopped flashing and turned white, as the gaps between the exploding shells closed to nothing, like the individual beats of a drum condensing into a single, deafening cacophonous roll. We could barely hear the screams and shouts of men scrambling to get underground.

'One by one we piled down the steps to the bottom, then along a tunnel past the officers' quarters to one of the rooms at the end. There we waited, watching the walls of our tomb for signs of subsidence, as the timber supports shivered uncontrollably, sneezing out dust that clouded the room. Kush stood by the exit, polishing his rifle with his gun-cloth, eager to face the enemy the moment the barrage ceased. I sat on a bunk next to Deepak and Dev, our rifles held upright between our knees. Facing us sat two farmers, both of whom had volunteered shortly after the outbreak of the war. Soon we would see what they had seen. Soon we would be their equals. One of them looked across at me.

'"Your friend looks as though he wants to go up there and wrestle the shells with his bare hands," he said, nodding towards Kush. Kush overheard him.

'"Down here, I feel like a rabbit hiding from the farmer," he told them.

'"Ha," said the other man, wagging his finger at the

ceiling. "That is one farmer you do not wish to tangle with, unless you want to find out how the neck of a corn stalk feels before a scythe."'

'"Or a clod of earth beneath a plough blade," added his neighbour. "I have seen a fragment of shell part a man in half like the perfect furrow."'

'The roar outside continued, sending shudders through the walls that threatened to bring them down around us. Some men prayed or checked their kit, whilst others worked in teams to strengthen the walls with planks ripped from our bunks. I wrote hurried letters home for several of the men. And then the pounding stopped, and we were back up top, splashing our way along the trench, weaving around the mounds of earth and wood that had caved in under the bombardment, and the shattered bodies of men who had not reached the dug-out. We had no time to help them, only to search for undamaged stretches of firing step on which we might raise ourselves up to repel the forthcoming attack.

'"Quickly, quickly, to your positions. Get ready."'

'And then, our firing positions secured, we waited for the enemy to set out across the muddy moonscape towards us, with little sound but that of the stiff breeze blowing in our faces. With Kush to my right and his brothers to my left, we were ready to meet the enemy face-to-face. They would fly at us, and we at them, and there would be a great battle. We would fight like lions, our valiant hearts bursting with gallantry and heroism. A roaring would fill the barren landscape as we tore at the enemy, fighting with tooth and claw, filling the air with the sound of clashing steel and, finally, the cries of victory as we sent them back to the holes from which they had crawled. For that was what we believed war to be. Instead, the enemy sent a vile, foul-breathed demon to do its dirty work. Other fellows described the cloud of gas as a blanket, unrolling over the ground to cover and suffocate us. But that is not what I saw coming towards us. I did not see an evenness. If the cloud was a blanket then I could see its individual threads, how they moved and intertwined and wove together like the wispy tentacles of a thousand ghostly squids, preparing to choke the life out of every living thing in their path.

'I confess to you now, Amil, that the sight of this giant beast that was about to engulf us froze my blood. I did not move. All around me warning bells rang and orders were barked. But I heard none of it. Neither did I see the men around me scrambling for their masks and pulling them down over their heads. I stood motionless, hypnotised by the roll and tumble of the pale green monster as it rode the wind towards us. I remember thinking, How could the wind be on the side of the enemy? Were we fighting the gods too?

'With a sudden gust it was upon us. Impervious to

bullet or bayonet, its tentacles reached into our trench. I felt one of them wrap itself around my neck, whilst others jammed themselves into my nose and mouth and down my throat, and pumped fire into my lungs. Still more attacked my eyes, stabbing at them with their chilli-hot tips until they too were on fire. I remember sinking to my knees in the mud, retching on all fours like a sick dog, my eyes welded shut against the heat. Then I felt a cold wet gun-cloth being pressed over my mouth and nose, and I was heaved backwards through the mud. Even though my eyes were tight shut, I had to see who had come to my rescue. So, I prised them open like slits, and peered out through a stinging watery haze. In that moment, I thought that I had died and been transported to some strange land. For I saw the face of a ghost, staring down at me through huge porthole eyes. And even though it did not have a mouth, the face spoke to me, and I heard Kush's voice.

' "You damn fool! Why did you not put on your mask? Do you want to spend the rest of your life as a blind man, begging on the streets of Bhopal?"

'I could not answer him, or even thank him. I could not speak. As the sound of machine gun fire erupted behind me, all I could do was close my eyes. And then they took me away.'

Suddenly, Sanjiv erupted into a cough; a rattling, shoulder-heaving cough so fierce that were it not for the thin layer of wrinkled flesh holding them together, his bones would have tumbled to the floor like a collapsing stack of cards. Eventually, the cough subsided and he sank back into the rags. Amil closed the journal and stared silently into the corner for a few moments. Then, he too, closed his eyes.

A few hours later, a loud creak from downstairs jolted him awake. Someone had opened the workshop door. He could think of no reason why it would be Mr Kumar or Chunni, and he had no desire to see Jalesh. Every bone in his body told him to stay put. There was nothing of great value down there. Whoever they were would soon leave. Then he thought of what Mr Kumar would say if he arrived the next day to find the table and chairs stolen. And what he would do. He had to investigate. He reached for his torch, finding to his dismay that he had fallen asleep with it switched on, reducing his reading light to nothing but a faint orange glow, like a miniature sunset. Silently, he slid out of the hammock. With a little help from the moonlight seeping in through the skylight he felt his way towards the hatch. He opened it a crack and peered down into the gloom to see Chunni wheeling the cart out of the workshop. By the time he had scrambled down she had closed the door behind her. He poked his head outside, but she was nowhere to be seen. The high moon told him that it was around midnight. He retraced his steps, leaving the hatch slightly ajar so that he might hear her return.

An hour later, he heard the cart coming back down the street. The squeak had returned. Peering through a slit in the window boards it was easy to see why. With her knuckles clamped tight around the handle and her body angled forward as though she were walking headlong into a hurricane, Chunni was pulling an abnormally heavy load. Hunched in the cart, with one hand dragging along the ground beside him and the other rising and falling on his belly as he snored, was Mr Kumar. Chunni drew the cart up outside the house and shook her father awake. She helped him heave himself up out of the cart and, with his arm lying heavily around her shoulders, led him to the door. Steadied against the doorframe and with no further use for his daughter, he brushed her aside and disappeared into the house. As Chunni headed towards the workshop, Amil raced back into the attic and watched her through a sliver of open hatch. Treading softly, as though she did not wish to wake him, Chunni returned the cart to the exact spot from which she had taken it, before creeping silently out of the building.

10

Dangerous Liquids

The next day, when Chunni brought Amil his breakfast, she suggested to him that it might be a good idea to check the wheels of the cart for squeaks.

'Just in case,' she said, 'you know what my father is like. If he hears the wheels squeaking after telling you to oil them, he will fly into a rage.'

Amil nodded his agreement, just as Jalesh appeared in the doorway.

'Hey, paper-folder. My father says that a very important job is due here today, and that you are to clean the workshop before it arrives. So get to it. If the room is not spotless when I return from school, I will make you lick the floor clean with your tongue.'

As he turned to leave, Chunni ran to the door.

'Did Pappa give you ten rupees for the chicken? Today is Friday.'

Jalesh glared at his sister, before taking a handful of coins from his pocket and waving them just beyond her reach, forcing her to jump for them like a performing animal. When he grew tired of that, he threw the coins at her feet, clucking and flapping his elbows as she scratched around on the floor to retrieve them like a chicken pecking seeds from the dirt.

'You look as though you are about to lay an egg,' he mocked. Then he left, clucking loudly until he reached the end of the street. Chunni stood up and dropped the money into the pocket of her dress, before brushing the dust from her knees. She and Amil exchanged glances, a shared, unspoken fear and loathing of her brother connecting them like an invisible cord.

'I have to clean the house and tend to my father,' she said. 'If you have finished cleaning by the time I return, you may come with me to the chicken shop.'

An hour later, she returned with an embroidered canvas bag slung over her shoulder, large enough to carry a chicken and anything else she might decide to pick up on the way. Having swept and cleaned the workshop floor and wiped down the trestle table, Amil was ready to join her. Together, they set off to collect a chicken for Mr Kumar's weekend curries. Mr Sharma's chicken shop was situated in the heart of the market, sandwiched between a shoemaker's and a bakery. In front, obscuring the view of the shop from the street, was a row of stalls selling everything from bags to bananas. Were it not for the bright yellow and red sign running across the top of the shop, most passersby would never have known it was there. But Chunni was a regular customer, and led Amil between two stalls directly to the front of the shop. There, across its width, a row of dead chickens hung by their feet according to colour; white chickens at one end, black at the other, with a range of brown and speckled birds in between. Amil stood inside the doorway as Chunni marched up to the counter, where Mr Sharma was tying the feet of a chicken together, ready to add it to the window display. He was about the same age as Chunni's father, but as scrawny as the chickens he sold. Amil noticed that, like his uncle Ravi, Mr Sharma had deep creases around his eyes which fanned out like crow's feet. He knew that in the case of his uncle Ravi these were caused by his constant laughing and joking. But, strangely, Mr Sharma did not seem at all jovial. In fact, as Chunni approached him, his face appeared flat and uneventful, like a drizzly day.

'Good morning, Mr Sharma. I would like to buy a plucked chicken please,' Chunni said.

Mr Sharma stared at her from beneath a pair of bushy eyebrows.

'There are no plucked chickens today, Chunni,' he replied. 'Mrs Sharma has sprained her wrist playing cricket for India. You will have to pluck the chicken yourself.'

Chunni held out nine rupees. 'The chickens are ten rupees,' Mr Sharma reminded her.

'*Plucked* chickens are ten rupees,' replied Chunni, placing the money on the counter, 'and please be sure to leave its legs on. My father likes to suck the feet.' Seemingly reluctant, Mr Sharma took Chunni's money and handed over the chicken. Then he took a step backwards and parted the beaded curtain covering the doorway behind him.

'You see,' he shouted upstairs to his wife, 'already your stupid cricket is costing me money!'

Chunni placed the chicken in her bag and turned to leave the shop.

'Good day, Mr Sharma.'

Mr Sharma winked at her.

'Good day, Chunni.'

On the way back from the chicken shop they took a detour to the Upper Lake. For a few minutes they sat in silence on a wooden bench admiring the view, and watching the herons take off and land. Chunni scanned the ground and retrieved several discarded lollipop sticks from the dust around a nearby litter bin. She dropped all but one into her bag. 'The tourists come here and leave them lying around,' she explained. 'I have collected hundreds of them. They are too small to sell to the recycler, but I am sure there must be a way to make money from them.' Amil watched her as she stroked the base of her plait to measure its length, before rolling it up and securing it to her scalp with the spare lollipop stick.

'I am growing my own crop,' she told him. 'When my hair is long enough for me to sit on, I shall cut it off and sell it to a wigmaker. Everything has a value. I even overheard my father telling his friends at the tea house, that he had agreed to cancel your family debt for a million rupees.'

Amil shook his head.

'I will never have that many rupees. Besides, it is a debt of honour, not money.'

Chunni disagreed. 'If he said it in front of a hundred people and repeated it at the tea house, he would have to honour his promise. Then you can see your family again. In any case, you are lucky simply to have a mother, even if you do not see her for the next eight years. I have never seen my mother, not even in a picture, and even if I live for a thousand years, I never will.'

Chunni pulled the bag on to her knees and wrapped her arms around it.

'All I have is this bag. My father sold everything else that belonged to her. He forbids me to use it but I do, whenever he is not looking.' She lifted it to her face and breathed in deeply. 'Sometimes, I hope that I might be able to smell her. But all I can ever smell is chicken.'

'Where is your mother?' Amil asked.

Chunni stared out over the water, as though she might be looking for her.

'She died when I was born,' she replied. 'Jalesh says it was my fault and that she would still be alive were it not for me. He says that is why I have to do all the washing and cooking and cleaning, and everything else that she would have done if she were alive, and why I cannot go to school.'

'Can your father not give you lessons at home?' Amil asked.

Chunni shook her head. 'He is always at the tea house,' she explained. 'He says that it is where all the "movers and shakers" of Bhopal go to do business. He says that if he does not go there every day there would be no food on the table. But I have never once seen Mr Panwar at the tea house, nor any of our other customers. They are always at their places of work. That is where I talk to them. That is where today's job has come from. Not the tea house.'

'What is a "mover and shaker"?' asked Amil.

'I think it is someone who gets things done,' Chunni explained.

'Then that is what you are,' said Amil, 'a mover and shaker.'

Chunni failed to recognise the compliment, having

never before received one. Instead, she stood up. 'We had better get moving then,' she said.

When they returned, Chunni went straight into the house to prepare lunch for her father. Amil let himself into the workshop to find it full of boxes, stacked in tall thin towers. He reached up on his toes to lift a box from one of them. The tower swayed as he dragged it off, but he managed to half-place, half-drop the heavy box on to the end of the trestle table, ready for folding.

'Careful, you clumsy idiot! You will dent the corners.' Mr Kumar entered the workshop. Even though he had surfaced from his slumbers, his eyes appeared still to be half-closed. 'Do you know what you are to do?'

Amil opened the box and took an unfolded leaflet from inside.

'Yes, Mr Kumar. I am to fold all the leaflets in half, like last time,' he replied, adding, 'with perfectly aligned corners and no smudges . . . or blood on them.'

'Correct. Even you should be able to manage that.' Mr Kumar walked back towards the door. 'You have four days to complete the job. That should be plenty of time.'

Amil looked up at the huge piles of boxes looming over him like an avenue of skyscrapers.

'Excuse me, Mr Kumar. May I have an oil lamp so that I might also work at night?'

Mr Kumar turned. 'Clearly, you do not have a business

brain,' he said, tapping his temple with a forefinger. 'Otherwise, you would know that every good businessman must minimise his overheads. That is why you use the hand-pump outside to wash, and why I have no intention of wasting expensive lamp oil on you, when sunshine is free. You will work from dawn until dusk. And in between you will do nothing but eat your meals and sleep, so that you are ready for work as soon as the cockerels crow each day. Is that clear?'

Amil nodded. With his torch battery flat, he had been hoping to read his great-grandfather's journal by the light of an oil lamp. Perhaps, if he finished his job early he might have time to go to the pesticide plant to get a new battery from his uncle. He emptied the first box of leaflets on to the table, and began folding.

The next few days seemed to merge into one. For Amil, the only difference between them was the movement of boxes in the workshop as, one by one, he emptied and folded the contents of each box to his left, before repacking it and adding it to the ever-growing pile to his right. Each day at dawn and dusk the hatch in the workshop door would open and a paratha or roti would be put through for him, accompanied, if he was lucky, by a small portion of daal. Each evening he would eat the food in silence, then retreat upstairs to lie in his hammock, hoping that he would hear his great-grandfather's voice in the darkness, or that a full moon might appear like a reading light in the sky, allowing him to read a few words of the journal. But neither came. So, he ate, and slept, and prayed to be reunited with his family, and all day, every day, he folded as fast as he could.

Occasionally, he would pause to experiment with his technique on leaflets that he considered smudged beyond use. In time, he found that he could fold a leaflet almost as perfectly with his eyes shut as he could with them open, albeit a fraction slower, and that he could fold a leaflet a dozen times from left to right so that each crease was perfectly parallel and equidistant to the next. He also discovered that he enjoyed folding a single sheet of paper in numerous directions, each time opening out the fold to create a matrix of rebounding lines and angular shapes, which fitted together like a perfectly assembled puzzle. Sometimes he continued folding, watching the paper age before his eyes as the crease lines on it multiplied and deepened, until they resembled the cracks and crevices etched into the face of his great-grandfather.

Even with these diversions, with a day to spare, he had finished. His neck and back both ached from sitting down for so long, and his eyes and fingers were sore from endlessly aligning corners and smoothing down creases. But he had done it. Every leaflet was folded. He emerged, blinking, almost happy, into the early morning sun just as Mr Kumar was leaving his house.

'I have finished, Mr Kumar.'

Mr Kumar frowned at him suspiciously.

'That was quick.' He strode into the workshop and delved into the nearest box, pulling out half a dozen leaflets for inspection. Then he picked a few more from another box, then another, then another. Each time his eyes grew wider and his mouth smaller, as his lips pressed ever tighter together. At the same time his body seemed to inflate, snorting air in short sharp breaths through flared nostrils until, as he reached the final box, he seemed ready to explode. There was a brief moment of calm as he stared down at the leaflets nestling in his hand. Then, slowly, like an archer drawing back his bow, he drew back his arm . . . and hurled the leaflets as hard as he could across the workshop. 'You have folded them the wrong way round!' He waved a leaflet in Amil's face, stabbing the pages with his finger. '*That* is supposed to be the front page! That is the back page! And those two pages should be on the inside! *Not* the outside!' He clasped his forehead. 'What is the matter with you, boy? It should have been obvious. Are you trying to destroy what is left of my business?'

He grabbed the arm of the chair in which Amil was sitting and yanked it out from under him, sending Amil sprawling on to the floor. Chunni and Jalesh came running to the doorway to find Mr Kumar standing over Amil, his fists raised, eyes bulging, cheeks bloated with rage. He turned to them. 'Do you know what this idiot boy has done? He has folded every single leaflet inside out.'

Jalesh clapped his hands slowly. Then he walked over to Amil and dragged him up from the floor by his hair.

'Please, Mr Kumar. I will do them again.'

Chunni stepped between Amil and Mr Kumar. 'Pappaji, if you beat the boy he will be unable to refold them. Then we will all have to redo the job ourselves.'

'I say give him the beating he deserves,' said Jalesh. 'The customer is expecting delivery tomorrow. He will not be able to refold them in time anyway.'

'He will if I help him,' said Chunni. 'You should not have to do this menial work yourself, Pappaji. You are a highly-respected businessman, not a lowly paper-folder.'

Mr Kumar unclenched his fist. For once, the girl was right. He nodded to her sharply, then pushed her aside to get to Amil. He leaned forward so that their noses were almost touching, and Amil could taste his smoke-stained breath.

'The next time I come into this workshop,' he growled, prodding Amil in the chest, 'every leaflet will be folded perfectly, or you will get the beating of your life. Do you understand?'

Amil nodded, his lips quivering, his eyes one blink away

from becoming waterfalls. Mr Kumar turned his back, muttering contempt for Amil's caste as he stormed out of the workshop. Jalesh sauntered after him, pausing only to smirk at Amil on his way out, whilst drawing a forefinger slowly across his neck. Then Amil blinked, and a reservoir of tears ran silently down his cheeks.

Chunni was unsympathetic.

'My father is right. You are an idiot. Next time, fold one leaflet for his approval before going ahead with the whole lot.' She lifted one of the boxes back on to the table and began to unpack it, stacking the leaflets in neat piles ready to refold. 'And wipe your eyes, otherwise the leaflets will be soaking wet as well as inside out.'

She sat down at the table next to Amil and pulled a pile of leaflets towards her. Then she set herself to the task, her back straight, her face grim with determination, her strong, nimble fingers working fast and accurately. Out of the corner of his watery eye Amil watched and copied, finding his own technique improving so that soon they were folding in unison, each edging the other towards greater speed and accuracy. Every half an hour or so, they would leave their seats to transfer piles of refolded leaflets back into their boxes, before unloading a new box and repeating the process.

As the light began to fade, Chunni returned to the house to prepare dinner for her father and brother.

Amil continued folding, pausing only to wipe beads of sweat from his brow or flex his fingers whenever they started to feel stiff.

Chunni returned an hour later with an oil lamp and two aloo parathas. She and Amil ate in silence, wiping their hands carefully before resuming their task. They worked through the night until, as the cockerels crowed across Bhopal, every leaflet had been refolded and repacked. Chunni made one last check, taking a sample from every box to ensure that it was correct, before placing four boxes in the cart ready for delivery later. Finally, she collected their empty plates and the oil lamp, and let herself quietly out of the workshop. Amil watched her go, grateful. For, despite her harsh words, he was in no doubt that Chunni had saved him from a terrible fate, just as surely as Kush had saved Sanjiv on the battlefield. How could his great-grandfather ever have betrayed him?

The rest of that day was just as exhausting as the last, but to Amil it felt like a holiday. He had woken to find his head on the trestle table and the backs of his legs stuck fast to the plastic chair in which he had fallen asleep. The door hatch had just slammed shut, drawing his attention to the small bowl that Chunni had pushed through for him. It contained an unusually meagre ration of cold and mushy rice, no doubt on the instruction of Mr Kumar, still eager to punish Amil for his mistake. And, of course, for being a Gujar. He ate the contents in two gulps, before licking Chunni's floury fingerprints from around the rim so that nothing was wasted.

Then Mr Kumar had swept in to examine the boxes. To Amil's relief he had merely grunted his approval and left, leaving him and Chunni with the day-long task of delivering them to the factory owner for whom they had been printed. She arrived a few minutes later, and they set off. Little was said as they trudged to and fro between the workshop and their customer. His factory lay on the other side of the city, and even though Chunni steered them through narrow, shaded alleyways to avoid the scorching heat of the main streets, their work was hot and exhausting, requiring them to suck water from every hand-pump on the way. After fearing for his life the previous day Amil was glad of the simple monotony of their task, and of the chance to help Chunni drag the cart up some of the steeper slopes. But she set a relentless pace, slackening it only when the last box had been delivered and she and Amil were on the final return journey. Then, for a few minutes before they went their separate ways, she and Amil were able to share the silent satisfaction of a job well done, albeit after a disastrous start.

When his uncle visited him in the evening, Amil could tell that he had not enjoyed the same sense of job satisfaction that day. As they sat on the floor, it was Amil who was in better spirits. He had already finished his dinner – barely larger than his breakfast – but his uncle had brought a can of fizzy orange for him. Amil, thirsty and still ravenous with hunger, opened it quickly and began gulping it down, enjoying the unfamiliar feeling of fullness as the fizz expanded inside his stomach. As he drank, his uncle talked.

'There have been more redundancies at the pesticide plant,' he told him. 'Now, I have to find the leaks *and* tighten the nuts and bolts, of which there are many, many thousands. I am like a fly, buzzing around from place to place, unable ever to stop and do a proper job. Standards will fall, mark my words. One man cannot do the work of two with equal efficiency. That is common sense, even though the general manager appears unable to see it! I have even written to him, but although he assures me that the matter will be looked into, no action has been taken. And yet every nut and bolt is vital, Amil. A badly fixed valve is as dangerous as a badly fixed lock on the cage of a man-eating tiger. In fact, it is a thousand times worse, because if gas escapes from the pesticide plant it will savage more people than a tiger ever could.' Uncle Ravi pointed a finger in the direction of the plant. 'There are enough chemicals in those storage tanks to kill every man, woman and child in Bhopal. Give me a tiger any day.'

'But I thought that pesticides only killed insects, not

people,' said Amil, tipping his head back to catch the last drops of fizzy orange on his tongue.

'That is true,' replied his uncle, 'but the chemicals they mix together to *make* the pesticides are deadly. It is rather like mixing boiling water and ice together. Mixed in the right quantities and stirred vigorously, the result would be a lovely warm bath in which one might relax in complete safety. But that does not mean it would be safe to dive into a tank of boiling water, or allow yourself to be encased in ice so that your blood freezes. In both cases you would die very quickly. And very painfully. That is why my job is so important. Because the chemicals in those tanks must be kept under complete control. They cannot be allowed to leak out through a badly fixed valve, or to mix with something they have no business mixing with. If they do . . .' Uncle Ravi expelled air from his mouth, miming an explosion that threw him back on the floor. For a few seconds, he writhed around clutching his throat as though it were on fire. Then he lay still, and staring, and for a moment Amil was reminded of the drawings of fallen soldiers in Sanjiv's journal. He leaned forward to shake his uncle by the shoulders.

'Chachaji, *Chachaji!*'

His uncle sat up and dusted off his overalls.

'That is what will happen if the gas escapes, Amil. So, if you hear the warning sirens, you know what you must do.'

Amil nodded. 'I must run like the wind.'

'Yes. But *even faster*,' his uncle replied. 'You cannot let it catch you.'

Uncle Ravi stood up to leave. Halfway out of the door he reached into his pocket.

'I almost forgot,' he said, 'here is another battery for your torch.'

Amil watched his uncle turn the corner at the end of the street. Then he returned to the attic and climbed into his hammock with the journal. But his eyes were heavy from the previous night's folding, and before he could turn on the torch, he had fallen asleep. He dreamed he was still downstairs at the table, folding. But this time he was folding a photograph of his family. They were smiling at him, waving, beckoning him to join them as they celebrated the Festival of Lights at home, surrounded by a glowing sea of Diwali candles. And then they would disappear as he folded the photograph in half. Then he would pick up another copy of the photograph and fold that. Then another. And each time he picked up a new photograph it was fainter than the last, so that his family were gradually fading to nothing. He tried to stop folding but his hands just carried on, folding and folding and folding until at last his family had disappeared and he found himself folding blank sheets of paper. And then, when there was no paper left to fold, he woke up.

11
Watching the Clouds

Amil switched on his torch and reopened the journal. He turned to a page that was filled with nothing but lines and squiggles.

'What is this, Pardadaji?'

In the gloom, his great-grandfather's head emerged sleepily from the rag pile. 'That is the part of my story that was recorded not by me, but by my pen,' he said.

'I do not understand,' said Amil. Sanjiv rubbed his eyes, before continuing.

'When they took me away from the battlefield the medics bandaged my eyes, stretching the cloth so tightly around my head that I could hear nothing but my own gurgling breath. Neither could I smell or taste anything but gas, the stench of which –' he sniffed twice – 'lingers in my nostrils to this day. In the absence of all my other senses, only the feeling of movement could distract me from the furnace burning in my eyes and lungs. The fire would have consumed my thoughts had I not set my mind on every dip and sway and jolt and turn along my journey to hospital.

I knew that, somehow, I had to record every moment of my adventures for my son – for I had no doubt that my wife would bear me a boy. So, even though I could not see to write, as I lay in the back of the field ambulance I took out my journal and pen, and drew my nib slowly across the page.' Sanjiv closed his eyes and ran a fingernail, like a long yellow pen nib, across the palm of his hand. 'My pen did the rest.'

Amil shone his torch along a jolting, tremulous line which every so often launched itself up, as though the pen inscribing it might shoot off the top of the page.

'Potholes,' Sanjiv explained. 'The ride to the field hospital was bone-shaking enough, but the driver seemed to steer the ambulance into every pothole on the way, sending my pen flying.' The next line was smooth and wavy.

'Did you catch a ship back to India?' Amil asked.

'That is a good guess,' Sanjiv replied, 'but the ship took me to England. Then, after a short train journey along the coast, we arrived at a place called Brighton.'

With his fingertip, Amil traced the next set of drawings: a row of spirals, like the fossil twirls of long-dead shellfish.

'Those are twists and turns in the road,' Sanjiv explained, 'as another ambulance weaved its way from the railway station to the hospital. Judging by the number of times I bumped my head, I think it must have had the same mad driver.'

Finally, Amil drew his beam along the last line on the page, a line which was as straight as any line could be without help from a ruler. Amil's great-grandfather sighed, and leaned back into the comfort of his rag pile. 'That line I drew in the stillness of my hospital bed,' he said. 'Oh, to be still at last.

'The nurses kept my eyes bandaged for many weeks. All that reminded me that I was alive was the burning in my eyes and lungs, and the desire to learn the fate of my friends, which burned in me no less fiercely. I could not bear the thought that having saved me, Kush and his brothers may have perished. And yet every attempt to enquire after their fate sent flames roaring into my throat, consuming my words before they could leave my mouth. Or so I thought. Somehow the nurses must have heard me and when, finally, my bandages were removed, they told me that Kush and his brothers were alive. I thought my day could get no better until, moments later, I slowly opened my eyes to the evening light. Then, for a moment, I truly believed that I had died and been reborn as a prince. For I found myself in a palace.' He emitted a raw, throaty chuckle, which turned into a cough. 'Me, Sanjiv Gujar. In a palace, no less. Can you believe that?'

Amil looked at the drawing which Sanjiv had made of

the building. Its towers, minarets and domes looked familiar.

'It looks a bit like the Taj Mahal,' he said.

'And yet it is not,' his great-grandfather replied. 'Look closely. You will find its name written underneath.' Amil brought the journal closer to his face.

'The Roy-al Pa-vilion, Brighton, England,' he read.

'That is correct,' said Sanjiv. 'I was living in a Roy-al Pa-vilion. Such were the honours bestowed upon humble soldiers like ourselves. There were hundreds of us, our beds laid in circles under the magnificent main dome, spreading outwards like ripples from the centre. Every Indian religion and caste was catered for, so that the food we ate and the way we prayed was as if we were still at home. For three months over the summer, while my body slowly purged itself of the gas, I would sit in the grounds of the Pavilion by morning, and after lunch walk to the beach to breathe in the clean air blowing in off the sea. With a few wiggles of my backside, the beach pebbles would mould themselves around my body, and I would lie there for hours cocooned in comfort, before returning for dinner.

'For a month after my bandages were removed, my eyes still burned like hot coals. So, often I would keep them closed, and listen to the crash and scrape of the waves pounding and retreating over the pebbles, whilst savouring the healing caress of the salty breeze against my skin. I liked to imagine that the wind brushing my arms had once kissed the cheeks of my wife as she hung out the washing, and would return one day to kiss my newborn child. For the wind has no beginning and no end, Amil. It just keeps going round and round like the currents of the ocean, touching us all.

'Gradually, as my eyes recovered, I spent more and more time staring up at the heavens, studying the clouds so that I might discuss the weather with the captain on my return to France. Over the summer, I saw many of the clouds that he had described to me, or that I had copied from his book. And when I was not looking up at the sky, I was looking down, searching among the pebbles for a lucky stone.'

'What is that?' Amil asked.

'A lucky stone is a pebble with a hole in it,' Sanjiv replied, 'like the one you found with my journal. In Brighton, many people believed that such pebbles had the power to ward off evil spirits. Local farmers nailed them to their barn doors to keep their animals healthy, whilst the fishermen carried them at sea to protect them against wind and waves, and help bring them a good catch. I cannot say that the one I found brought me much luck, even though I kept it around my neck. But it had another, far greater use.'

Amil's eyes widened. 'Better than bringing good luck?'

His great-grandfather nodded. 'Whenever I was alone,' he said, 'I would use the pebble to transport myself to another world.'

Amil's mouth dropped open. 'How is that possible, Pardadaji?'

Slowly and stiffly, Sanjiv looked to his left and right, before leaning forward slightly and lowering his voice.

'First, I would close one of my eyes. Then, with the other I would stare at the sky through the hole in the centre of the pebble. Sometimes the view was so sharp and intense that it blanked out everything around me, every other sight, and sound, and smell. For a time, nothing would exist except that little patch of blue, and the shapes of the clouds floating through it. It was like peeping through a keyhole into another world, one in which men did not fill the air with poison, and where hot metal was used to forge the words of poets, not fly through the air like invisible scythes to cut them down. Sometimes, if I pressed the pebble tight to my eye and looked through it hard enough, I could feel myself squeezing through the hole into the world beyond. And there I would stay, until someone touched me, or a seagull squawked in my ear.'

'I think you were very lucky to see into other worlds,' said Amil. 'I think it was a lucky stone after all.'

'Perhaps you are right,' agreed Sanjiv. 'But I did not always like what I saw. When I looked through the hole at sunset the clouds were hot and red, as if created by the raw angry strokes of a brush dipped in men's blood. Then, they became the flames of burning buildings, or huge avenging faces boiling with crimson rage, and I would find myself transported back to the battlefield. I rarely stayed to watch the sun go down.

'As the summer progressed and the temperature rose, I would sometimes remove my tunic to let the cool wind wash over me, tipping my head back and sucking in the clean sea air to remind myself that the wind did not always taste of death. I never tired of gazing up at the clouds, or of watching the seagulls draw endless patterns in the sky.

'In time, I began to see a connection between the stately ebb and flow of the clouds and the twists and turns of the seagulls below them. They were connected, like puppets attached to the same set of strings, the movement of each controlled by the same puppet master – the wind. To understand the movement of the clouds was to understand the movement of the wind and everything it controlled. In time, I found that I could predict every wheel and turn of the seagulls – each tilt of their wings like an individual word leading me fluently to the next, as though they were the words of a poem that I had read a thousand times. When I realised that it was not the minds of the seagulls that I could read, but the movement of the wind, I widened my studies. Before long, I could predict each curl of grey smoke rising from the pipes of the fishermen, the airborne antics of children's Sunday kites; even the passage of souls less fortunate than me billowing up from a military funeral pyre on a nearby hillside. For a long time I thought nothing of it, and on some days, when the sky was particularly overcast and the air cool, the gulls seemed to have a mind of their own. Only after a few weeks did I realise that it was on the hottest days, when I removed my shirt and could feel the wind brushing the hairs across my body, that the wind spoke to me directly, as though Vayu himself was whispering in my ear. On those days I could see it, and hear it, and understand it as clearly as you can understand me now.'

'I am not sure I do understand,' said Amil. 'How can anyone read the wind?'

'Not just anyone, Amil. You and me. It is a gift we share. Go to the window and I will show you.'

Amil jumped out of the hammock and on to the trunk. He peeled back the plastic sheet covering the skylight and felt the cool air brushing his face and arms. He turned back to his great-grandfather, whose voice rasped quietly from the shadows.

'Amil, can you tell me what my next word is going to . . .' He paused.

'Be?' Amil said.

'You see. You understand my language. You recognised

the pattern of my words and knew exactly what I was going to say next.' He tapped the side of his head with a spindly forefinger. 'You predicted the future. Now, imagine understanding the language of the wind in the same way. Imagine knowing how it will move from one place to the next, bouncing and reflecting off everything that lies in its path: the buildings, the trees, the lampposts, the people. When you understand how the wind moves between them, you will be able to read its intentions as clearly as you can read the pages of my journal.' The old man slumped back against the wall, wheezing.

'Can you teach me . . .'

'. . . how to do it?' Sanjiv interjected, grinning. 'I think, perhaps, that is why I am here. Hold your arms up to the wind and tell me what you see?'

'I see thousands of tiny black hairs,' Amil replied. 'I have so many that my mother used to call me her little bear cub.'

'Now look closer, Amil, then closer still – see how they move, like a field of long grass bending and swaying in the breeze, or perhaps a bank of seaweed twisting and turning in the ocean current. Feel the hairs rippling and swaying as the wind draws ever-changing patterns on your skin. These are its words. The wind is talking to you. Now look out. See how the clouds are for ever changing shape as the wind moulds them to its will, see how the burning embers of the cooking fires in the slums twist and turn as they rise, how the smoke from them billows this way and that as the wind weaves its way around the streets. There is a connection between what you can see out there, and what you can feel against your skin, Amil. When you can join the two together, you will be able to read the wind and predict its course.'

'Why does my father not have this gift, or my uncle Ravi?'

'Perhaps they do, as they are both Gujars,' Sanjiv replied. 'But neither has been taught how to use it. You will be the first.'

'How long will it take? Does it not take many years to learn a language?' Amil asked.

His great-grandfather shook his head.

'The language is inside you already, like a dormant memory – you simply need to nudge it awake.'

Amil looked out of the skylight. The moon had just risen and embarked on its long arc across the sky, shining through every passing cloud to reveal its secrets. Lower down, beyond the columns of smoke twisting upwards from numerous cooking fires, great billowing spouts of steam, illuminated by the lights of the pesticide plant, squeezed like escaping genies from vents and valves dotted around the site.

'The wind connects them all,' Sanjiv told him. 'By the

morning, you will be able to see how.' As he spoke, a bat flew past Amil's ear and disappeared into the night. His great-grandfather clapped his hands with delight.

'You will be like that bat,' he said. 'You will be able to see what your eyes alone cannot. Now, shall we begin?'

Amil removed the plastic from around the skylight and tucked it temporarily behind the trunk. Then he took off his shirt and spread his arms and fingers wide. One by one, with his great-grandfather whispering instructions to him from across the room, he studied the clouds as they sailed in front of the moon like a flotilla of ghostly ships crossing an inky sea. As the night passed, each one revealed to him a little more of his gift. And as with any gift the more he saw of it, the more he recognised what it was, and the quicker he wanted to tear away the wrapping and use it. By the time the moon reached the top of its arc, his skin was tingling with excitement and anticipation. By the time it had surrendered to the dawn, the gift had revealed itself to him. All he had to do now was master it.

12

Seeing the Wind

Swish-whack . . . swish-whack. Amil could hear Chunni outside, beating a tired old rug to within an inch of its life with a broom handle. The rug hung from a line strung between the house and the workshop, and appeared to contain an endless supply of dust. *Swish-whack . . . swish-whack.* At each strike the rug would double-up like a man punched in the stomach, and cough a huge cloud of grey dust into the morning breeze. Passersby were not at all pleased.

'Out the way, girl, you are choking me to death!'

'Mind that stick, you nearly took my eye out!'

'Be careful, you are covering my clothes in dust!'

Amil stood bleary-eyed by the workshop door, watching the air move as Chunni continued cutting through it with her stick. *Swish-whack . . . swish-whack.* He could feel it being pushed out of the way as the stick swished through it, then curl back on itself to fill the empty space left in its wake. He could feel it shudder as the stick whacked the rug, and dust exploded outwards like a cloud of microscopic shrapnel bursting from an exploding shell. But, most of all, he saw patterns. He saw them not only in the twists and curls of the dust clouds, which were visible to anyone who cared to look, but in the clear, invisible air beyond as it danced to the rhythm of Chunni's beat. So transfixed did he become watching the dance being performed around him, that he could no longer hear the rug being struck, or the protestations of the passersby or, indeed, Mr Kumar calling to him from across the street. Suddenly, a shoe hit him in the chest. He fumbled to catch it, finally succeeding just before it hit the ground.

'Wake up, boy. Today, you will help Chunni run some errands.' Mr Kumar stepped to one side as his daughter carried the rug back into the house. 'First, you will go to the shoemaker to get my shoes restitched. They are barely two years old and already they are falling apart like wet cardboard. Remind him that I am a very influential businessman in Bhopal, so unless he wants his reputation to disintegrate as fast as his shoes, he had better repair them free of charge. After that, the two of you will collect the money that Mr Panwar owes me for the last paper-folding job, and remind him that currently we are offering the services of two paper-folders for the price of one. Whilst you are about it, you can give our other customers the same message; you will have plenty of time.' Amil caught the second shoe as it sailed over the street, narrowly missing the head of a passerby. 'And be sure the shoemaker polishes them; I cannot attend business meetings at the tea house wearing filthy shoes.'

He returned indoors just as Chunni re-emerged into the sunlight. She crossed the street to join Amil.

'Bring the cart,' she said.

At the shoemaker's shop, Chunni tried in vain to negotiate a deal for the restitching of her father's shoes, settling instead for an assurance that they would be ready and polished by the time she and Amil returned to collect them later that day. Mr Panwar was more helpful, paying Chunni what he owed and allowing her to take away several bags of inky rags and wastepaper. These she sold at an assortment of recycling shacks on their return journey, during which she disappeared into numerous businesses to announce Kumar and Sons' latest sales offer. The proceeds of the recycling allowed her to buy a small sack of flour and pay for the shoe repairs without dipping into the money Mr Panwar had given her, every rupee of which she knew her father would expect to put into his pocket.

Throughout the day, Amil had been content to follow a few paces behind the cart. Normally, he would have been eager to help, constantly asking Chunni if he might share the load, or accompany her inside the recycling stations. But, today, his head was in the clouds. Today, he spent his time watching smoke rise from the small cooking fires on each street corner, and observing how dust and fumes from passing traffic swirled between buildings, and even how steam curled up from teacups on the tables outside the tea houses. Occasionally, he would close his eyes and listen to the hairs on his arms as they informed him of every twist and turn, and every change in speed and direction of the wind blowing across his skin. His first attempt had ended with a painful yelp, as one of his shins collided with the cart, which Chunni had brought to a sudden halt in front of him.

'What on earth are you doing?' she had asked him.

'Practising,' he had replied, rubbing his leg vigorously.

'Practising what, breaking your shins?'

'Walking with my eyes closed,' Amil replied, not knowing how to explain the truth.

Though puzzled by his reply, Chunni stifled her natural curiosity. She had work to do; business to conduct.

'Then walk alongside the cart, not behind it. I cannot afford to drag you around in it all day with two broken legs.' Then she had leaned forward and continued on her way.

Having completed the day's errands, Amil returned to Chunni's side and they headed back to the workshop, jointly pulling the cart which contained nothing now but the bag of flour and Mr Kumar's shoes. As they turned into Chunni's street, suddenly she quickened her pace, as though eager to get home. But instead of returning to her house she strode past it without a sideways glance.

'Where are we going?' Amil asked, trotting to keep up.

'I do not like an empty cart,' she told him, 'It is like an empty lorry, wearing out its tyres, using up its oil and petrol and paying the wages of its driver without earning a single rupee. If we are quick, we have time for one more errand.'

At the end of the street they continued on into the slums, weaving their way through the seething mass of rotting shacks which lay like an open wound between them and the pesticide plant beyond. But Amil did not notice the decay around him. Instead, his eyes were fixed on the pesticide plant in the distance, drawn like a moth to a flame by the brightness of the future it represented – a future in which he, Amil Gujar, wore a uniform and a helmet, and waged war against the bugs that had for so long wreaked havoc on his country. At last, he was getting closer. Twisting and turning through the slums, he smelled nothing, heard nothing, saw nothing, except the huge silver storage tanks rising like sentinels into the sky, casting their long shadows over the people of Bhopal. Finally, just beyond the outer edge of the slum the ground fell away in a steep slope, so that by the time they reached the pesticide plant's perimeter fencing at the bottom, only the crest of the slope was visible behind them. The slums, and the noisy, teeming life that inhabited them, might just as well have been a thousand miles away.

For a few seconds, Amil curled his fingers around the fence wire and peered eagerly inside. Then his arms dropped limply to his side. His uncle was right. Seen up close, the plant was not the space-age wonder it had appeared to be from the top of the telegraph pole, or even from the skylight in the Kumars' workshop. It was a mirage. On closer inspection nothing gleamed or sparkled as he had expected it to. In many places silver had given way to creeping rust-red whilst the sharp, linear edges of the concrete walkways had grown soft and fuzzy with weeds. Even the wire fence, which looked straight and seamless from the top of the slope, was a patchwork of make do and mend, much like the slums through which they had just walked. Even Chunni, who was a regular, albeit unofficial, visitor to the plant, seemed taken aback.

'There are more holes in the fence than ever,' she told Amil. 'I think they have given up repairing them.'

'Why have we come here?' asked Amil.

'You will find out soon enough,' Chunni replied, bending down to examine a hole that had been patched up with string. She unravelled the repair in seconds. 'The cart will not go through. You will have to stay here and guard it while I go inside.'

'Like a sentry?' asked Amil.

'What is that?' replied Chunni.

'Someone who keeps watch,' he said.

'Yes, like a sentry. Watch the cart and make sure no one steals it. Or my father will kill us.' Chunni tucked her hair into the back of her dress. Then she crawled under the wire and jumped up on the other side. 'There are more weeds than last time, too,' she observed, looking around her feet. 'Everything is getting worse.'

A few feet away from her, a tap stood at the top of a long copper pipe extruding from the ground. A decaying house sparrow lay at the edge of a small puddle which had accumulated beneath it. Chunni turned on the tap.

'What are you doing?'

'What do you think I am doing, Amil? I am taking a drink of water. My mouth is parched.'

'You cannot drink from there.' Amil pointed to a small sign attached to the pipe. 'It says, *Do not drink*.'

'Who cares? No one is watching!' said Chunni, cupping her hands beneath the tap.

'The sign is not saying the water is private,' said Amil. 'It is saying it is poisonous. Look!' He pointed to the dead sparrow. 'And the puddle has a funny-shaped rainbow floating in it. I can see it from here.'

Chunni hesitated, sniffing the water flowing over her hands. 'But I have drunk from this tap before.'

Amil's mouth dropped open. 'Well, you cannot drink

from it now. Everything in this place is dangerous. My uncle Ravi told me.' Suddenly, Chunni was not quite so thirsty. The water had tasted a bit . . . metallic last time, she remembered, like sucking an old spoon. And she had suffered from a tummy ache afterwards. She turned off the tap.

'I will be as quick as I can,' she said. Then, she set off towards the maze of tanks and pipework. Amil waited until Chunni was out of sight, then sat with his back resting against the cart. Having been awake all night, he was tempted to curl up inside it, to close his eyes just for a few moments. But he knew he could not risk falling asleep. He was on sentry duty, after all. Instead, he watched the hypnotic *drip, drip, drip* of the tap. Even though Chunni had turned it off, it had continued to leak, slowly replenishing the puddle at its base. Clearly, this was one valve which his uncle had not had time to check. He watched as another sparrow fluttered down on to the tap. It perched there, flicking its head this way and that as it examined the drip beneath its feet. Amil did not want it to die too. He leaped up and shooed it away, but it returned, again and again. And he knew it would return the moment he and Chunni had gone. Perhaps he should try to stop the drip. He squeezed under the wire and with both hands tightened the tap as much as he could. The drip slowed, but did not stop. All he could do was ensure that no sparrow poisoned itself whilst he was there. So, he squatted on his heels by the puddle. Shielding his eyes from the sun, he passed the time watching the dust swirl around in the wind between the storage tanks. Then, as the wind picked up, he watched the dead sparrow's loose, fluffy brown feathers detach themselves from its body one by one, and take flight, dancing to its tune. Somehow, the pattern of their movement seemed familiar to him, as though he had seen their dance before. But he knew that was impossible. Instead, he realised that he was predicting their movement. He could see where each feather was going before it got there, and knew every last tuck and dive and pirouette that it would make along the way. Sanjiv was right, they shared a gift. Like his great-grandfather, he could not only see and understand the movement of the wind. He could predict it.

Chunni reappeared, running towards him across the weed-infested concrete. Her face was hidden behind a huge bundle of uniforms, the arms and legs of which were flapping in the wind so that she appeared to be locked in combat with a giant blue octopus. Behind her, another uniform – this time with a security officer inside it – was lumbering after her. Instinctively, Amil ran to help, taking several of the uniforms from her so that she could see where she was going. Together, they ran towards the hole in the fence. Chunni reached it first, bundling the uniforms through the gap before squeezing after them and throwing them into the cart. She turned back just in time to see Amil trip over a clump of weed. As the uniforms spilled into the air, a gust of wind pressed them into the wire, freezing them in demented human shapes. Amil jumped up and began frantically piling them back into his arms, like washing from a clothesline at the onset of a storm. He pushed them through the hole to Chunni, before crawling after them. Halfway through, the back of his shirt snagged on a piece of wire, pinning him to the ground.

'Chunni, *Chunni!*' The man was only a few yards away now, and Amil was caught like a fish on the end of a hook. Chunni rushed to him, delving into the folds of cloth until she found the end of the wire. Calmly, she unhooked him and yanked the fence up, dragging Amil to safety just as the man made a grab for his ankles. They could still hear him panting as they climbed the slope with their haul. Then, as they reached the top, the din and sweat of the slum washed over them like a breaking wave, and sucked them back into its midst.

They did not stop running until the workshop doors were closed firmly behind them. For a few moments they slumped in the chairs and said nothing. Amil noticed that Chunni's eyes were red and watery.

'You are crying,' he said.

Chunni rubbed her eyes.

'I am not crying. My eyes are stinging, that is all.' She

126

leaned over to examine the tear in Amil's shirt. It was nothing a few stitches could not fix. Even so, they had had a narrow escape. 'Next time you must stay outside the wire, like I told you,' she said. 'You could have got us both caught.'

'I do not want to do that again,' Amil replied. 'It is wrong to steal.'

Chunni glared at him.

'We did not steal anything, Amil. The uniforms had been thrown away in the rubbish bins. Anyway, what if I had stolen them? Would you rather starve? Where do you think your breakfast comes from every morning?' She stood up. 'I will get some scissors from the house so we can cut them up. If the ragman knows where they have come from, he will try to negotiate a lower price.'

While she was gone, Amil began to sift through the uniforms, looking for any that might once have fitted his father. Perhaps one of them bore his father's name on a tag inside. Perhaps one might even smell of him. He pressed one of the uniforms to his face and took a deep breath. Instantly, the smell made his eyes smart and the back of his throat sore, as if a thousand miniature claws were scratching at it. He threw the uniform back on the cart and waited for Chunni by the open doorway, gulping back the clean air and resisting the temptation to wipe his watery eyes. Instead, he let them well up, hoping that when the tears fell, they would wash away the soreness. Thoughts of his family, so far away, soon contributed to the flow, so that by the time Chunni returned Amil's cheeks were streaked with tears. At first, Chunni pretended not to notice. Then she turned to him. 'Tears do not pluck chickens, Amil. Or fold paper. Or make rags.' She handed him one of the uniforms. Amil wiped his eyes and together, holding each uniform at arm's length, they set about transforming them into rags. Chunni cut. Amil ripped.

'It is a shame we do not have some other rags to mix with these,' Chunni said when they had finished. 'The ragman is not stupid.'

Amil thought of the pile of rags upstairs, and of Sanjiv. But he said nothing.

13

The White Feather

That night, shortly after Amil had picked up the journal and started reading, Sanjiv's head emerged from the rag pile. Amil sat up, grinning.

'I am . . . jubilant!' he said.

Sanjiv chuckled. Then his shoulders began to heave as his amusement turned into a bone-shaking cough.

'Jubilant, indeed,' he rasped, recovering himself. 'And why is that?'

'This morning, I watched Chunni beat a carpet outside in the wind. I knew exactly where the dust would blow, Pardadaji. Every time she hit it. And later, I did the same thing watching a sparrow flying around. Even before it tilted its wings I knew where it would go!' His great-grandfather nodded his approval, as though Amil's gift had never been in doubt. Then he tipped back his head and sniffed the air.

'What is that disgusting smell? It is making me feel giddy.'

'Rags,' Amil explained. 'There is a cartload downstairs which Chunni and I are taking to the ragman tomorrow.'

Sanjiv sniffed again, short and sharp, as though he was suspicious of what the air might contain.

'There are some smells which are very hard to get out of your nostrils,' he said. 'Death is one of them. Poison gas another. My nostrils have been full of both. Even when I was convalescing on Brighton beach, breathing great lungfuls of sea air every day, the smells remained, and with them the memories of all the death and destruction I had seen. I needed to keep busy, so that I did not spend my time thinking about the battlefield.'

'What did you do, Pardadaji?' Amil asked.

'I volunteered to write letters home for my fellow patients, even though my eyes still stung if I kept them open for long.'

'Did they pay you?' Sanjiv nodded.

'They paid me in cigarette cards. I sent them home to young Mani, who collected them. His favourite set featured portraits of Indian war heroes, which were also very popular among the men. On one occasion, I had been sitting on the beach, propped up against the promenade wall beside a farmer for whom I was writing a letter. He was being sent back to the front, despite having lost two of his fingers. His letter to his wife was a most sorry affair, warning her that he was unlikely ever to return to her unless he had several limbs missing. This was not an uncommon complaint among my fellow soldiers, who felt that to be injured in battle was to have honourably fulfilled their duty and should have earned them a passage home. He paid me in the usual way, handing me a cigarette card which depicted a soldier by the name of Darwan Singh Negi. He asked me to describe the illustrious soldier's exploits, so I turned the card over to read the back. *"With two wounds to his head and one to his arm,"* I told him, *"he led the fighting along a trench which had been captured by the enemy, braving bombs and rifle fire at every turn until the last of them had been cleared out. For this he was honoured,"* I continued, *"with the Victoria Cross, the highest award for gallantry in the British and Commonwealth forces."*

'The soldier looked down at his bandaged hand.

' "That is all very well," he said, "but what use is honour if I am dead, or broken in half? Will honour till the soil or plant the crops? Will it put food in the mouths of my children?"

'I had no answer for him, so he had turned his back on me and left. I remained on the beach, listening to the hypnotic crash of waves in front of me, and the clickety-clack of English ladies' heels on the promenade above. The words of the soldier troubled me. Was honour more important than returning home whole, so that I could feed my family? What would happen to the Kumars and their business if the three brothers did not return, except perhaps as pictures on the front of some cigarette cards?

'I lay back on the pebbles, suddenly feeling very tired, and gazed at the sky, looking for inspiration, as though the answers to my questions might be floating there. The sky was clear, but for a light feathery cloud directly above me. It reminded me of a giant feather, or a horse's tail blowing in the wind. From my pocket, I retrieved the journal you are holding, in order to find its name. Sure enough, I had seen it in Captain Bradbury's cloud atlas and drawn my own picture of it. It was called a mare's tail, or to give it its proper name, *cirrus uncinus* – a fine, stately name for a horse, I thought. I remember pressing the lucky stone to my eye, obscuring everything around me so that I could see nothing but the mare's tail through the hole in its centre. It was stirring slowly in the wind, as though it were being flicked gently by a beast just beyond my view. Deeper and deeper into the hole I peered as if, somehow, I might catch a glimpse not just of the mare's tail, but of the mare itself. And then, suddenly, I was on the other side of the hole, as though I had been fired through a tunnel and shot out the other side. I jumped to my feet just as a magnificent white horse swooped out of the sky towards me, its huge feathery wings spread wide as it arced on the wind. As it swept past me, I grabbed hold of its mane and swung myself on to its back. Then up, up, up it went, wheeling out to sea before turning inland to circle high above the majestic onion domes of the pavilion, glinting in the sun like the temples and palaces of Bhopal.

'What a ride it was! As it tilted its wings back towards Brighton seafront, mothers pushing their prams gazed up in wonder, whilst children ran along waving to me, and soldiers saluted. For in my uniform, I must have looked for all the world like a winged cavalry officer. As seagulls flew alongside like royal outriders, I clung on tight, clenching my fists around the horse's mane. The wind coursed over me as the magnificent beast rose and fell through the sky in wide sweeping circles, like the fairground ride of the gods. And then the horse glided lower, spiralling gracefully to circle, silent and unnoticed, above an old woman. She was walking slowly along the promenade, her eyes fixed straight ahead, the thin white feather clutched between her fingers almost luminous against the blackness of her dress. Approaching her from the opposite direction was a young man. He was about my age, but wearing a workman's overalls and cap instead of a military uniform. A shovel was slung over his shoulder in place of a rifle. As they met, he touched his cap politely and stepped to one side. But the old woman stepped in front of him, barring his way. Then she thrust the feather into his hand and spoke to him through tight angry lips. Her jagged words were sucked away by the wind before they could reach me. But I remember the young man appearing to shrink as she uttered them, as though they were pressing down on his shoulders, crushing his bones, squeezing the breath out of his lungs. When, finally, he walked on, a jittery hand having pushed the feather out of sight into his pocket, his legs seemed barely able to carry the extra burden.

'How could the feather of a bird be so heavy? I had thought to myself. How could such a bird ever fly? In a few moments he was gone, shrunk to nothing, leaving just the feather tumbling along the promenade in the breeze. For a moment, I closed my sore eyes against the wind, only to open them back on the beach with the sea lapping at my feet, and a cloudless sky above. Of course, when I returned to the hospital I told no one about the white horse. But I did describe the encounter between the old woman and the young man. The nurses told me that by handing him a white feather, the old woman was branding him a coward because he was not in uniform, fighting for his country. I vowed then that I would never have to shrink under the gaze of an old woman. When I returned to the trenches I would fight like a lion; I would protect my comrades and bring great honour to my family. For I had seen with my own eyes how a man without honour can cease to exist, just as surely as if he were killed in battle. My son would be able to walk through the streets of Bhopal with his head held high. "There goes the son of Sanjiv Gujar."'

Amil closed the journal. 'Was it all a dream,' he asked, 'The horse, the old woman, the young man with the shovel?'

'How would I know?' replied Sanjiv. 'I was asleep at the time.' Amil laughed. 'All I know is that it was better than the nightmare that was to come,' his great-grandfather continued. 'Besides, who can say what is real and what is not? Have you considered that I may be no more than a figment of your imagination? Induced by all the strange vapours emanating from the bottles on those shelves, filling your head with giddy imaginings? Or perhaps the words in my journal are weaving a magic spell, conjuring up their author before your eyes? Have you thought of that?'

Amil had. And more. Indeed, he wanted everything to be a dream – not just Sanjiv, but the attic, Mr Kumar, even Chunni. Each day he would pinch himself hard, hoping that he would wake up to the smell of his mother's cooking. Yet each day the nightmare continued, until he was forced to conclude that this new life was indeed real. Sometimes, alone at night, he would do his best to shut it out. He would curl up into a tight ball in his hammock, swaying weightless and untouched. With his eyes squeezed shut and his hands clamped over his ears, he would breathe through the merest crack in his lips so that no taste, nor sound, nor smell from the nightmare in which he found himself could enter him. Instead, he would float there, neither alive nor dead, awake or asleep – safe for a few moments in a world that had nothing in it but his silent prayers. And then, as now, he would fall asleep.

14

A Bullock's Backside

The following day, as shafts of morning light began their daily passage across the workshop, Uncle Ravi paid an unexpected visit.

'We are undermanned at the plant today, so I have to get in extra early. I have brought some parathas from your auntie Maya. She says to tell you that they were made with love, as well as flour.' He handed Amil a cloth bundle, warm and pungent from the buttery, freshly-baked flatbread inside. 'One each,' he said, squatting down.

They lay the cloth between them and nibbled at their breakfast. There was no particular news of Amil's family, but Uncle Ravi assured him that they were well. Amil had even less to report. He could hardly mention his scavenging trip to the pesticide plant. Despite Chunni's assurances, he felt that their visit was tantamount to a criminal escapade, the knowledge of which would make his uncle very angry with him, and his parents, if they knew, deeply ashamed. Neither did he wish to mention his newly discovered gift, not least because he knew it would sound fanciful. For the same reason, he could not talk about Sanjiv, whose friendly familial presence in the attic his uncle would, almost certainly, consider to be nothing more than a wishful mirage. Instead, there was a question that he was burning to ask.

'Do you ever think about the wind, Chachaji?'

Uncle Ravi's face froze for a few seconds, as though Amil had stumbled across a deep, dark, secret that he had expected never to discuss. Then he resumed chewing.

'All the time,' he replied. 'Who could not? There is nothing more important to us. The wind dries our washing and brings us the monsoon rains so that our crops will grow. It brings us some of the world's greatest pleasures, like the smell of jasmine, or a freshly-cooked Bhopali curry.'

'Or you, Chachaji!' Amil joked.

'Exactly. And what kind of world would it be without kites, and clouds moving across the sky pulling faces at us? The wind brings us all of these things, with the finesse and power to ruffle our hair one moment, and suck us into the sky the next. Who could not think about the wind?'

'Do you think it is alive?' Amil continued.

'Of course it is alive,' his uncle replied. 'Does it not wail like a baby? Can you not hear it whining like a complaining child, or sighing like a lovesick teenager, or roaring like a soldier plunging into battle?'

Amil wanted to know more. He wanted to know whether his uncle was like him, and his great-grandfather.

'Do you like the feel of it on your skin?' he asked.

His uncle took a mouthful of paratha, chewing over Amil's question.

'Sometimes . . . when my skin is hot, and the air is cool.' Then his eyes seemed to light up. 'But most of all, I like the music it makes. When I was your age, I would lie awake at night listening to it whistle and howl through the city, turning everything it touched into a musical instrument, from the high-pitched soprano squeak of a swinging shop sign, to the percussive rhythmic power of a banging shutter. One by one the sounds would gather in my head, until I could hear them merge into a single piece of music, a magnificent symphony being played just for me.' Uncle Ravi smiled. 'Since I have worked at the plant, I have discovered an entirely new repertoire. When I put my ear to the pipes I can hear them hum as the wind courses over them, each note decided by the twists and turns and thickness of the pipe, and the strength of the wind as it caresses or howls across the metal. Even the wires in the perimeter fence vibrate in the wind like mile-long sitar strings.' He reached into his pocket and pulled out his torch. Then, holding it delicately between his thumb and forefinger, he closed his eyes, and with it began slowly to draw invisible figures of eight in the air. 'I have not told this to anyone before, not even your father,' he said, 'but sometimes, on the nightshift, when the wind blows across the plant creating melodies in the pipework and harmonies in the fencing, I will climb to the top of the tallest storage tank and use my torch to conduct the wind as though it were a great orchestra – the orchestra of Vayu.' He opened his eyes and returned the torch to his pocket. 'Why did you ask me about the wind? Do you have a draught coming in through that hole in your shirt?'

Before Amil could reply, his uncle rose to his feet. It was time for him to go to work. But Amil did not mind. For now he knew that his uncle Ravi, and almost certainly his father, shared his gift. They were simply not aware of it. One day, he would pass Sanjiv's teaching on to them. And, in the meantime, the wind connected them, as it connected everything.

As the sound of his uncle's footsteps receded, the hatch slid open and a pair of floury hands delivered a small round paratha – his second breakfast of the day, albeit less generously spiced and buttered than the first. He ate it quickly, eager for the day's work to begin. Once he and Chunni had sold the rags, they were to spend the day collecting boxes of leaflets from Mr Panwar, a big order that would take most of the day to collect, and most of the week to fold. Even though the sun was unseasonably fierce for November – still almost hot enough to fry an egg on the top of Mr Kumar's head – Amil was looking forward to another day walking to and fro across the city, away from Mr Kumar and Jalesh, and angry security guards.

Chunni arrived a few minutes later and, together, they pulled the laden cart to the rag merchant's shack.

Amil watched from the doorway as Chunni wheeled it inside. She pressed her hands together and nodded towards the centre of the room.

'Good morning, Ragman,' she said.

'Good morning, Chunni.' The voice came from a pyramid of cloth, behind which a pair of spindly arms were fast at work, sifting, sorting and throwing individual rags on to various piles situated around the room. Absorbent rags, durable rags, wearable rags, rags for wiping, rags for stuffing, white rags, coloured rags; there was a pile for each, and every shred of cloth found its way on to one of them, thrown in a blur of pinpoint accuracy by the ragman's dancing hands. 'What have you brought me today?' he asked.

'A full cartload,' Chunni replied. 'Cotton and colourfast, nothing but the best.' The ragman jumped to his feet. He was as ragged and threadbare as his surroundings, except for his beard, from which hung numerous ribbons of chequered and spotted and brightly coloured cloth, mementos cut from some of the finest rags he had encountered over his long career.

'That is a fine haul you have there, Chunni,' he said, sifting through the cart. 'Let me see. All good quality cloth. All quite new. And all very blue. And what is this, a sleeve? And here, a leg? And here another sleeve? And here another leg? It is as though someone has taken a dozen pairs of overalls from the pesticide plant, and cut them into small, rag-sized pieces.'

Chunni could see where the conversation was leading.

'Do you want to buy them or not, Ragman,' she said briskly. 'There are other rag merchants in Bhopal.'

'I will give you fifteen rupees for them,' the ragman said. 'Not a single rupee more.'

'But that is half what you normally pay me for a cartload,' Chunni protested.

'And double what anyone else will pay you for these, Chunni. I suggest you accept my offer. Otherwise, I might feel compelled to inform the plant that you have been trespassing again.'

Chunni tipped the rags out of the cart and took the ragman's money.

'I hope all the buttons fall off,' she said, turning to leave.

'That would be a delight,' the ragman replied. 'It would save me a lot of bother.'

Outside, Chunni showed Amil the collection of tiny coins nestling in the palm of her hand. 'A pittance,' she observed, shaking her head bitterly. 'This is barely enough to buy a can of cooking oil. There must be a better way than this to earn money.'

The trip to Mr Panwar's printworks was even more disappointing. Mr Panwar greeted them cheerfully enough, but he had bad news.

'There are only four boxes of leaflets for you to fold, Chunni.'

'But my father told me I would be collecting at least twenty,' Chunni explained. 'He said they are instruction leaflets to go inside boxes of pesticide.'

Mr Panwar shrugged. 'That is right. But the pesticide plant cut the order at the last minute. I was as surprised as you are. They are not selling enough boxes of pesticide, you see, so they do not need as many instruction leaflets to go inside them. It is all due to the recent drought, I am told. Because of it the crops have not grown, so there have been no pests to kill, which means the farmers have not bought any pesticide. Worse still, with no crops to sell, the farmers will have no money to buy seed for next year, even if the rains return. So then, even less pesticide will be sold. Soon every business in Bhopal will have queues of starving farmers knocking on its doors asking for work.' He shook his head, 'And I have nothing else for you today, Chunni. I am sorry.'

Mr Panwar went back to tending one of his machines,

leaving Amil and Chunni to load the cart. They worked in silence for a few moments. Then Chunni put her hand on Amil's shoulder.

'Do not worry about your family. Your uncle has a good job at the pesticide plant. He will make sure they do not starve.' Amil nodded, happy to accept Chunni's reassurance, even though he suspected that his uncle's job at the plant was no safer than his father's had been. With time on their hands, they walked slowly away from Mr Panwar's and, as it was Friday, headed towards Mr Sharma's chicken shop. Amil stood outside guarding the cart, whilst Chunni went inside. He could hear her voice, flat with disappointment and worry.

'Good morning, Mr Sharma. I would like to buy one plucked chicken, please.'

'I am afraid there are no plucked chickens today, Chunni. The Queen of England is visiting us, so Mrs Sharma has been too busy to pluck anything. You will have to pluck the chicken yourself.'

Chunni held out nine rupees.

'The chickens are ten rupees,' Mr Sharma reminded her.

'*Plucked* chickens are ten rupees,' replied Chunni, placing the money on the counter, 'and please be sure to leave its legs on.' With a long theatrical sigh, Mr Sharma scooped up the money and handed over the chicken.

Then he poked his head through the doorway behind him, and shouted up an unseen staircase: 'You see, already the pair of you are costing me money!'

Chunni turned as she left the shop. 'Good day, Mr Sharma.'

Mr Sharma smiled at her. 'Good day, Chunni.'

With its new feathery passenger perched on top of the boxes, Amil and Chunni pulled the cart homeward in silence, whilst Amil tried to make sense of what he had just overheard. His mother and father had always told him that he had a vivid imagination. Yet somehow he could not quite imagine that the Queen of England would visit Mrs Sharma. On the other hand, he would never have imagined that one day he would be living with Mr Kumar, or for that matter, having conversations about the wind with his uncle. Halfway back to the workshop they stopped to drink from a hand-pump on the edge of a small square. Afterwards, they sat on the low shady wall beside it and watched some younger children playing cricket amid the noisy hustle and bustle of people buying and selling, meeting and greeting, and buzzing around on scooters. Finally, Amil broke the silence between them.

'Do you think the Queen of England is really upstairs at Mr Sharma's chicken shop?' he asked.

'Of course not!' said Chunni. 'And Mrs Sharma does not play cricket for India. He is just trying to make me smile. Two weeks ago he told me that Mrs Sharma had been swallowed by a giant boa constrictor. That did not work either. I told him that if he wishes to make me smile, he will have to sell the chickens to me for five rupees.'

'Why do you not want to smile?'

'I do,' she replied. 'But the first time I smile I want it to be for something . . . special.'

'Like what?' asked Amil.

'Like a half-price chicken! Or,' she hesitated, uncertain whether to trust Amil with her deepest yearning, 'or, my father saying thank you to me. He has never done that, not once, even though every day I cook and clean and make sure there is enough food to eat. Sometimes, I tell myself that it is because he is so forgetful. But I have heard him say it to Jalesh many times, even though he does nothing but skip school and hang around on street corners with his ruffian friends. One day, after I have saved up enough money to buy back our printing press, I will help my father restore the family business to how it used to be. First, we will start printing leaflets instead of merely folding them. Then, I will save up enough rupees to buy another machine that cuts the leaflets. And another that folds and stitches them. Soon, our workshop will clatter even louder than Mr Panwar's and we will be one of Bhopal's most successful printing companies again. My father will say it to me then; I am sure of it.' Her eyes dropped to the ground, scanning it for lollipop sticks. Amil was reminded of the gift that he had brought with him. He retrieved it from his pocket and handed it to Chunni.

'This is for you.'

'What is it?' asked Chunni.

'It is a fan. It was easy to make. I just folded a leaflet in a zigzag all the way across, then glued a lollipop stick to each end, and tied them together at the bottom with a piece of string.'

Chunni opened the fan and wafted it in front of her face, closing her eyes so that her eyelids might also benefit from the gentle breeze that it generated.

'It is to keep you cool when you are delivering boxes,' Amil told her. Chunni closed the fan. She turned it over in her hands, examining it closely before placing it carefully in the cart.

'Thank you,' she said. She did not smile as Amil hoped she would. Instead, she lifted the chicken on to her lap and began to pluck out its brown-speckled feathers. 'I have done this job every Friday since I was five years old,' she told Amil, 'and fetched water from the hand-pump every morning, and cooked dinner every night. Every day is the same; I know what I will do, and where I will go. Sometimes I wish I were one of these feathers. They never know where the wind will take them.'

'I do,' said Amil, 'I know exactly where they are going.'

'That is impossible,' Chunni said, throwing a handful of feathers at him. The wind blew them straight back in her face. 'And I suppose you knew that would happen too, did you?' she said, spitting a feather from between her lips. Amil nodded, smiling.

'I can prove it to you, if you like,' he said.

She plucked a single feather from the neck of the chicken and handed it to him.

'Go on then, if you think you are so clever.'

Amil removed his shirt and placed it on the wall beside Chunni. Then he took the feather from her.

'I will land the feather on the back of that bullock,' he told her, pointing to a tethered beast on the far side of the square. Before she could reply, he had turned his back and walked away. After a few paces he stopped, and slowly turned full circle to observe the sky, and the size and shape and position of everything else around him. For just as one might examine the contours of a stream to predict how a twig might travel along it, so Amil knew that he could drop a feather into the wind and predict every dip and twist and tumble in its path. Most importantly, for today's demonstration, he could tell where it would come to rest. When his eyes had told him what he needed to know, he closed them, stretching his arms out wide to feel the soft breeze whispering its intentions to the fine downy hairs on his skin. Finally, he was ready. He opened his eyes and took one last look at the unsuspecting beast. Then, holding the feather between his thumb and forefinger, he turned it to face the wind, took a small deliberate step to his left, and let it go.

At first the feather dropped towards the ground, as though it were too small and insignificant for the wind to bother with. But, at the last moment the wind appeared to change its mind, swooping down suddenly to scoop the feather up in its invisible hands. Chunni leaned forward, narrowing her eyes to stay focused on the feather as it floated out over the square, all the time gaining height until it was just a dark speck hanging in the sky. For a moment, she thought it would continue over the buildings on the far side, but then it began to circle, like a vulture lowering itself slowly towards its prey. As it descended, a cowbell jangled as the bullock looked up briefly, seemingly aware of the attention being lavished on it from across the square. Then, as it returned to its meditations, the feather finally came to rest, settling like a giant speckled fly on its backside. It did not remain there for long. With a swish of the animal's tail, it was returned to the wind and was gone. Chunni's eyes remained fixed in wonder on the bullock's behind until Amil returned to sit beside her on the wall. He was shaking his head with disappointment.

'I need to practise,' he told her, pulling his shirt back over his head. 'I was aiming for between its shoulder blades, not its backside. I think it would have been easy if nothing but the wind was moving, but there are so many people milling around.'

Despite Amil's disappointment, Chunni was impressed.

'But you were so close,' she said. 'How did you do it?'

'It was not too difficult,' he replied. 'The wind on the animal's back has to arrive from somewhere else, and it has to follow a path to get there. All I did was drop the feather into that path, that is all.'

'Where does the path start?' said Chunni.

'Nowhere,' said Amil. 'The wind has no beginning and no end, it just moves around the world, endlessly.' He thought of Sanjiv standing in the surf on Brighton beach: 'Like the currents of the ocean.'

They sat in silence for a moment. Then, Chunni plucked another feather from the chicken and handed it to Amil.

'Try again,' she said. So Amil began to practise his new skill, releasing feather after feather after feather whenever the square seemed most alive with the movement of people and their vehicles. In this way, as Chunni slowly plucked the chicken bare, he learned how the wind would deflect around any moving thing in its path, whether large or small, earthbound or airborne. By the time the owner of the bullock led his beast away, to Amil and Chunni's delight, he was able to hit any target perfectly, and without fail.

15

Return to France

'You would have made a good sniper,' his great-grandfather told him when he returned to the attic that night. 'If you can take account of the wind to hit your target with a feather, imagine how easy it would be with a bullet.'

'Did you become a sniper?' Amil asked him.

Sanjiv shook his head.

'I could do exactly what you can do. But even though I was a soldier about to return to the battlefield, the idea of taking pot shots at the enemy never crossed my mind. All I thought about was joining my friends and fighting alongside them. When I returned to France, I rejoined my company along with a score of new recruits. Arriving from England, I was freshly polished and preened, like them. But unlike them, I knew something of what awaited us. Kush and his brothers had volunteered to collect us from the town and escort us to the front line. Like the soldiers who had first escorted us, there was a gulf between them and the new men, not just in their outward demeanour but

151

behind their eyes; what they had seen, and what they were yet to see. I felt somewhere in between the two. In No Man's Land. Whilst I had come under fire and been injured, I had not fought like Kush and his brothers. I had not stared into the face of the enemy. I had not killed a man.

'As we marched back to the trench Kush described how, as the medics took me away, a strong wind blew up from the east, sucking the gas out of the small section of trench it had infiltrated, and dispersing it as quickly as it had arrived. Captain Bradbury had rallied our men, and they had waited. The enemy, who had been following behind the gas, continued towards us, only to find that their bombardment had failed to blow enough holes in our barbed wire defences for them to progress any further. Half-blinded by their masks, they could neither cut nor find a way through. Hundreds found themselves tangled in the wire, caught like flies in a spider's web, barely able to see the machine guns that were about to mow them down. They say it is easier to kill a man when you cannot see his eyes. According to Kush, the farmers along the line saw the Germans in their long dark-snouted masks not even as men, but as an infestation of giant bug-eyed insects; abominations of the field that needed to be eradicated. Their machine guns blazed white hot, spraying death on to the teeming hordes until few survived. Those that did, retreated in disarray, their attack a costly failure. My comrades owed their lives to the wind that day. And I, of course, owed mine to Kush.

'Not until we arrived back in the trench did Kush tell me that we had a new captain. Captain Bradbury had survived the battle, and the endless shelling that had continued whilst I had been in England. But he had been killed by a sniper's bullet the previous week, waving to an aeroplane flying overhead. When I arrived, an orderly took me down to the dug-out to meet his replacement. He was still moving in, packing up the captain's belongings for dispatch to England, whilst unpacking his own. He greeted me in Hindi, but thereafter the orderly translated for him. He was a boy, younger even than us, with a slightly plump face like a rosy apple. He knew nothing of India, or of us, and appeared stiff and ill-at-ease even in the comfort of his own quarters. As I turned to leave, he unhooked Captain Bradbury's hammock and handed it to me. He would not be needing it, his orderly explained, nor would the former captain's mare, who had been reassigned to another officer. I was welcome to drop it into one of the braziers. I did not, of course, otherwise you would not be lying in it now. Instead, when I emerged from the dug-out, I rolled it up and tied it to the bottom of my backpack.

'Around one of those braziers the following day, the young captain, accompanied by his orderly, delivered news of a forthcoming attack. The major general in command of our stretch of the line, he told us, had decided that now we were back to full strength we would launch our own assault on the enemy at the earliest opportunity. However, he was adamant that we would not make the same mistakes that they had made earlier in the year. The major general had decided that we too would use poison gas, but that our attack would be launched only when the wind was true and steady and would not turn. Our barrage on the enemy trenches beforehand would be twice as brutal, and last twice as long, as the one we had endured, destroying many of them in their dug-outs and cutting wide passages through their barbed wire. Once the gas had cleared beyond their trenches, we would advance in the clear air behind it, surging through the gaps unencumbered by masks. There, we would engage what was left of the enemy. His news dutifully delivered, the captain and his orderly had left. Kush and his brothers were jubilant at the prospect of avenging Captain Bradbury. But the stench of gas returned to my nostrils, and I could feel my insides burning again. Only this time, they were burning with anger.

'"What? No masks! That is madness!" I told them. "The wind does not make promises. If it wants to turn, it will turn."

'"That may be so," Kush said, "but the new captain is not about to argue with the major general, any more than our comrades from the country would question the wisdom of their village elders. He is young. He will follow his orders to the letter and expect us to do the same."

'"I think the major general should pay a visit to Brighton," I told them. "He should see all those poor fellows lying blind in their hospital beds. You saved me from the gas just in time, Kush. But some of them were not so lucky. Some of them ended up on the funeral pyre, and many others will never see again."

'"Visiting the hospital would make no difference," Kush said to me, "not if he truly believes that the wind can be trusted. In that case, he is right to think that we will fight better without our masks. Once the gas has passed over the enemy trenches, those who manage to crawl out in their black snouts will be facing us half-blind. I, for one, cannot wait to avenge our fallen comrades. If the major general is right, it will be a glorious victory."

'"But what if he is wrong and the wind changes course, Kush, what then? He is taking a terrible gamble with our lives."

'Kush stared into the fire. "Even so, we have to follow orders," he said. "Our honour depends on it." As he spoke, I remembered the young man being handed the feather on Brighton promenade, and how he had shrunk with shame until he had disappeared altogether. Kush was right. Without honour we are nothing. Yet I knew that honour could not be found solely by following orders.

'"What if the orders themselves are dishonourable," I said. "What if they are dishonest, or reckless, or cruel? Surely, true honour can only be found in the purpose for which one fights."

'"That may be so," he replied. "My purpose is to bring honour to my family, my caste and my country by proving myself equal to any warrior on the battlefield, including our British counterparts. If you are here because India has been promised independence in return for our loyalty and courage, then that, too, is honourable."

'That is when I realised that, in our own ways, Kush and I were fighting for the same thing.'

Sanjiv yawned, so Amil closed the journal and let his great-grandfather sink slowly back into his pile of rags. He did not mind the silence. For the wind spoke to him now, in a language that he understood more and more clearly with every passing moment. He moved to the skylight, ready to practise using his new gift. When he peered out he smiled. For in the darkness, above one of the storage tanks inside the pesticide plant, a light was dancing around like a demented firefly. Chachaji.

16
Betting on the Wind

When Amil and Chunni had returned from Mr Panwar's printworks with four boxes instead of the twenty that he had been expecting, Mr Kumar was in no doubt where the fault lay. His nostrils had flared as he sucked in the air around him, puffing himself up like a balloon ready to burst.

'That Gujar boy! Our customer must be dissatisfied with his workmanship. There can be no other explanation.'

But there was, and he had seemed to deflate before their eyes as Chunni explained to him that Mr Panwar was, in fact, perfectly happy with Amil's work, but could do nothing about the drought and its consequences for the pesticide plant, or for them. Mr Kumar had stormed out of the workshop, doubly annoyed at the sudden loss of that week's income, and his inability to blame Amil for it. At least, directly.

Over the next week, Amil barely saw Mr Kumar. He remained in his house during the day, unable to face either the blistering heat or the need to support his family. Only in the relative cool of the evenings did he venture out, dragging himself wearily to the tea house as though he had just completed a hard day's work. There he would stay until midnight, before falling into the cart that would be waiting faithfully for him outside. As his daughter pulled him home, the streets of Bhopal would echo to the sound of an unlikely duet as his low baritone snore joined the high falsetto squeak of the cart's over-burdened wheels.

Chunni may have spotted Amil peeping through the attic hatch as she returned the cart to the workshop every night. But clearly she had no wish to discuss her late-night trips. So, each morning, when she suggested again to Amil that the wheels could do with a dab of oil, he retrieved the oil can and returned them to smooth running order without comment. She, in turn, spared him the content of the conversations that she overheard whilst crouched outside the tea house, waiting for her father. As he sat in a circle, connected to a captive audience plugged like suckling pigs into the nozzles of a communal hookah pipe, he would recount the history of his family. Night after night, between puffs on the pipe and swigs from a bottle of liquor cradled between his legs, he would describe how the decline in its fortunes lay squarely at the cowardly feet of the Gujar family and its latest, useless descendant. A boy who – he never tired of repeating – was long overdue for a beating. When the subject of his own children arose Chunni would cover her ears, unable to bear her father's constant praise for Jalesh – 'Such muscles, if only I had more strapping sons like him' – and his total disregard for the loyal chauffeur, waiting nervously in the dark menacing shadows of the backstreet just a few feet away.

So, Chunni's midnight missions to the tea house were never mentioned. Instead, each day, she and Amil would spend an hour or two folding leaflets together, before finding an excuse to wheel the cart into the Old City in search of rags or anything else they might sell. Several times they saw Jalesh loitering on the streets with his friends and would duck into the nearest alleyway to avoid him. The same was true at the workshop, and on more than one occasion Amil hid in the attic when he heard Jalesh approach. For the older boy had nothing but contempt for Amil. He was a Gujar. Worse than a cockroach. And Amil had no wish to be stamped on. So he retreated to the attic whenever he could, emerging only to the sound of Chunni calling him, or of food being put through the hatch in the workshop door.

Every day, he would pick up Sanjiv's journal and settle into his hammock to begin reading. But the pages spoke only of routine, of catching sleep and keeping rifles clean, and Sanjiv would not emerge from the rag pile. So Amil's eyelids would begin to droop, and he would put down the journal and instead jump on to the trunk to stare out of the skylight. There, with the wind brushing the hairs on his skin, he would watch the steam billowing from vents in the pesticide plant, and map the course of numerous smoke trails as they rose from small cooking fires dotted around the slums. Occasionally, he would fix his gaze on a bird in flight, or a plastic bag as it danced in the wind, breathing in and out like a gossamer-thin lung. As it moved through the air his eyes would move with it, neither leading nor following, but joining, confident and unhesitating, as one might sing along to a well-known tune. And then he would return to the hammock and read a few more words. Somehow, he felt that, like his great-grandfather in the trenches all those years ago, he was waiting. But, for what, he did not know.

On Thursday night, as Chunni wheeled her father back from the tea house, she slipped ten rupees into his pocket. After lunch the following day, he emerged from the house as she was outside hanging up washing. Her father retrieved the coins from his pocket, raising his eyebrows slightly as if, for once, fortune had smiled on him. He handed them to his daughter.

'That is for the chicken,' he said. 'Never let it be said that I do not provide for this family.' Then he turned unsteadily on his heels and headed back into the house. 'And remember to leave its legs on!'

Leaving her father's shirts billowing like sails on the

washing line, Chunni went in search of Amil. She found him in the workshop with the cart on its side, dabbing oil on to the axle of each wheel as he spun it round. She rattled the coins in her hand.

'Are you ready to go to Mr Panwar's?' she said. Amil nodded, tipping the cart back into an upright position. Together, they loaded it up with the four boxes of folded leaflets and wheeled it, squeak-free, out of the workshop. They walked slowly, taking turns to cool themselves with Chunni's homemade fan. Zigzagging through narrow shaded alleyways, they tried to avoid the worst of the heat which, in the open, pressed down on them like a hot steaming flannel.

The pace had slowed at Mr Panwar's printworks too. For once, as they entered his workshop they were not greeted by the deafening hiss and clatter of industry, but by nothing more than the gentle swish of a broom, as Mr Panwar swept the floor alone. He put the broom aside and walked over to greet them, the first time ever that Chunni had heard his footsteps.

'The lull before the storm,' he joked, seeing Chunni survey the hive of inactivity. 'At least, I hope that is what it is. The pesticide plant has cancelled several orders this week, including that one,' he continued, pointing to the cart. 'They say the leaflets are no longer needed.' He reached into the pocket of his overalls and handed Chunni half the money that was due for their work. 'They have paid me only a small cancellation fee, so this is all I can give you. But you may sell the wastepaper to make up the difference. I am sorry, Chunni.' Mr Panwar returned slowly to his broom, and resumed sweeping.

At the chicken shop, Amil stood guard over the cart whilst Chunni went inside and approached the counter.

'Good morning, Mr Sharma,' she said, fanning herself gently. 'I would like to buy one plucked chicken, please.'

'There are no plucked chickens today, Chunni. Mrs Sharma is suffering from heatstroke. You will have to pluck the chicken yourself.'

Chunni held out nine rupees. For once, Mr Sharma accepted the money without protest, and handed her a scrawny white chicken by its legs. Neither did he call up the stairs to admonish his wife. Chunni felt short-changed. As she parted the beaded curtain to leave the shop she felt the sudden heat from outside burning her face, as though she had opened an oven door. She turned to Mr Sharma.

'Does Mrs Sharma really have heatstroke?' she asked.

Mr Sharma pressed his lips together and nodded.

'She is not at all well, Chunni. She is tired and sick and dizzy, and her skin is on fire. She cannot keep cool.' Chunni returned to the counter, and placed the paper fan in front of Mr Sharma. Then she returned to the doorway.

'Good day, Mr. Sharma.'

Mr Sharma smiled at her. 'Good day, Chunni.'

Outside, Chunni took the handle of the cart from Amil.

'Are we going to sell the paper, now?' he asked.

'I have a better idea,' Chunni replied, 'I will tell you about it when we get back to the workshop. First, let us go to the square again – it is shady there and my mouth is parched.'

Having quenched their thirsts in the square, they sat down in the same spot from which Chunni had witnessed Amil land a feather on to a bullock's backside the week before. For a few minutes, they watched the people and their animals come and go. Then, Chunni lifted the chicken on to the wall between them and began to pluck it. Amil noticed that this time, rather than scatter the feathers to the wind, she was stuffing them into the pocket of her dress. When all its feathers had been removed she placed the chicken back on the cart. Then she took the rupee left over from its purchase and held it out to Amil. He did not take it.

'Why are you giving me money?' he asked. 'For the next eight years everything I have belongs to your father. My uncle says so.'

'I will not tell him, or Jalesh,' Chunni replied. 'You can start saving the million rupees that my father said would release your family from their debt. Then you will be free, Amil. And if you have a son, he will be free too.'

'I will never have a son. Besides, your father was only making a joke for the crowd.'

'Even so, he would have to keep to his word. He said it in front of many witnesses, and repeated it to his friends. You should start collecting as many rupees as you can. The first rupee is from me.' Amil looked down at the coin nestling in the palm of Chunni's hand.

'Your father will have to eat a million chickens,' he said.

'There is another way,' Chunni told him. 'You can throw chicken feathers for bets. If I had been rich, I would have bet a million rupees that you would not be able to land the feather on the backside of that bullock. There is not a person in Bhopal who would believe such a thing possible. We can part them from their money, Amil.' She waved a white feather temptingly in front of his nose. 'It would be easy.'

'Taking money from someone who has earned it honestly is wrong,' said Amil.

Chunni disagreed. 'What if it is the only way for you to restore the honour of your family, and the only way for me restore the fortunes of mine. Do you want me to spend the rest of my life folding paper and collecting rags?'

Amil shook his head. 'Of course not,' he said, 'but still it would be wrong to make them lose their money.'

'What if they *enjoy* losing it,' Chunni replied, 'like all those people who fill the gambling dens on Friday nights. What if, for them, it is entertainment – would you deprive them of that?' Amil remained unconvinced, but Chunni persisted. 'They may lose their money, Amil. But it would be in return for the entertainment that you would provide, like buying a ticket to the cinema.'

At that moment, a tall man wearing a white safety helmet walked by on his way to the pesticide plant. As he retrieved a handkerchief from the back pocket of his overalls, a rupee fell into the dust behind him. Amil raced to retrieve it.

'You dropped this, sir,' he said, handing it back to him. The man nodded gratefully to Amil, then turned to continue on his journey, only to find Chunni barring his way. She looked up at him.

'Sir, would you like to make a small bet with that coin?' she said. The man hesitated. 'You have already lost it once, sir,' she reminded him. 'A few seconds ago whilst it lay in the dirt you did not possess it at all. Through good fortune it was returned to you. Perhaps the same good fortune will smile on you again.' The man took a step forward, but Chunni stood her ground. 'Alternatively, as my friend found the rupee and returned it to you, perhaps you may reward him with the chance to win it from you.'

'I do not want a reward,' Amil told her. 'Besides, if I lose any money, your father will beat me.'

'He will not beat you,' Chunni assured him, 'he is not expecting any change from the chicken money.' She took a white feather from her pocket and stepped towards him, brandishing it like the old woman in Sanjiv's dream. 'Are you too scared to try?'

Amil snatched it from her. He had no wish to shrink like the young man on Brighton promenade. 'I am not a coward,' he said, 'and I will prove it to you.'

The man looked at his watch. He still had time, and a rupee was neither here nor there. He turned to Amil. 'If you win the bet you may consider it a reward for your honesty,' he said. 'Now, I presume you have a rupee to match my own.'

Chunni held out Mr Sharma's change. 'One rupee.'

The man smiled. 'Then what is your bet?'

'I will bet you one rupee that my friend can throw that feather into your safety helmet from ten paces,' Chunni replied.

'That would be impossible, as I am wearing it,' the man joked. 'Do you mean like this?' He removed his helmet and placed it on the ground in front of him. Chunni nodded. 'Then, I believe that to be equally impossible,' the man said.

'Perhaps you are right,' Chunni replied, 'you are welcome to try for yourself first.'

The man took the feather from Amil and stood directly over his safety helmet, intending to drop it straight down. Then, he licked his forefinger and held it aloft. Detecting a slight breeze he took a pace backwards then, upon further deliberation, one pace more. Finally, he let go of the feather. The moment it left his grasp the wind blew it up his sleeve. Undeterred the man made a second attempt. This time he squatted over the helmet to shelter it from the wind. Then, he dangled the feather no more than an inch above it, and let go. Instantly, the wind whipped the feather straight up past his face, and carried it over a nearby rooftop. Chunni plucked another feather from her pocket and held it out to the man. He shook his head.

'It is impossible. Give it to your friend,' he said, nodding towards Amil. 'I will accept your bet.'

Amil removed his shirt and left it folded on the wall. Then, he took the feather from Chunni, and walked ten paces into the wind. As the air gently caressed the fine hairs on his back he twisted and turned his arms, feeling it weave its way around and between his splayed fingers. Every few paces he would stop to tip his head back, closing his eyes to sniff the air, like a bloodhound searching for clues. The ten paces took him to a nearby lamppost. He placed the feather between his teeth and climbed halfway up. Hooking his legs around the pole he took the feather from his teeth, closed his eyes and leaned backwards, arms outstretched as though he were imploring Vayu to grant safe passage to the feather. Then, just as he had done the week before, he turned the feather between his thumb and forefinger, made a final adjustment to its launch position, and released his grip. This time the feather travelled straight up, higher and higher until it could no longer be seen.

The man laughed and held out his hand to Chunni.

'You appear to owe me one rupee,' he said, 'and I sincerely hope that you have learned your lesson. I think you would have had more chance betting that a pig can fly.'

But Chunni was not listening to him. She was searching . . . And then she saw it.

'It is coming down again. Look, there it is . . .' She pointed into the clear blue sky above, where a soft fleck of white, like a faraway cloud, was descending slowly. The man looked up too, as did several onlookers, curious to know what he was staring at. Soon a small crowd had gathered to watch the feather descend, pondering its significance. As it came within grasp they moved back, eager to let the feather complete its journey undisturbed. Below it, the safety helmet lay like an open mouth, ready to swallow it whole. For a moment, as the feather approached the end of its journey it hung in the air, as though suspended by an invisible thread. Then, it dropped silently into the upturned helmet. As the onlookers moved on, bemused, the man stared open-mouthed at the feather nestling inside it.

Chunni took the money from his open palm. 'Thank you, sir,' she said, and ran to meet Amil at the foot of the lamppost.

When they arrived back at Kumar and Sons, Amil wheeled the cart into the workshop, and Chunni disappeared into the house to prepare that evening's daal and give her father the bad news about the unwanted leaflets. Whilst she was gone, Amil unloaded the cart and returned it to its position behind the sink, should Chunni need it later that night to collect her father from the tea house.

She returned two hours later, her fingers stained yellow with turmeric. She handed a small portion of daal to Amil, and sat with him whilst he ate it. Her father had taken the money Mr Panwar had given her, she told him. But he had been angry that she had not already sold the unwanted leaflets for scrap. 'He told me to sell them without delay and left for the tea house without waiting for his meal. I expect he will be trying to drum up some new business,' she explained.

Amil nodded in agreement. He continued eating, looking up from his bowl every few seconds to see Chunni watching him, as though she were trying to decide whether or not she could trust him. Finally, as he licked his fingers clean, she reached into her pocket and pulled out a bulging plastic bag. 'I want you to look after this for me,' she said, dropping it with a metallic clunk in front of Amil. 'It is the money I have been saving to buy back our printing press. I have been hiding it in the house, but it is no longer safe there.'

'Why not?' Amil asked.

'Because of some stupid cigarette card that was left to my father by his grandfather,' she explained. 'He says that there is someone who will pay a fortune for it. So he is always looking for it, even though he lost the card before Jalesh and I were born. Now he is threatening to rip the house apart brick by brick to find it once and for all. If he finds this money, he will spend it at the tea house. Besides, Jalesh is always searching my room for money to gamble away with his friends.' She removed a coin from the bag and offered it to Amil. 'This is the rupee you won today, fair and square. Will you take it this time?' Amil nodded. Chunni dropped the coin into his hand, and he placed it in his pocket.

'Where have you been hiding the money?' he asked.

'Behind a loose brick next to my sleeping mat. The other day I saw Jalesh notice that it was loose, so I asked him to fix it. That got rid of him, but he will be back when I am not there, and next time he may look behind it.'

Amil opened the bag and looked inside.

'There are hundreds of rupees in here!' he said.

'Three hundred and fifteen,' she told him. 'My father has eaten a lot of chickens, but most of it is from selling rags. Either way, if they find this money, I will be beaten for concealing it from them. But they will not look here. They know that you have nothing.'

In the attic after Chunni had left, Amil opened the trunk and took out Sanjiv's gas mask. Having twisted the top of the plastic bag several times to seal it shut, he placed it carefully inside the mask. Then he returned the gas mask to the trunk, dropped his own rupee alongside it, and closed the lid. It might take him many years to collect the one million rupees he needed to restore honour to the Gujar name, but he had made a start.

17
Chain of Command

Late the following morning, Mr Kumar appeared in the doorway of his house, scratching his chest. 'Chunni, where are you? Where are my roti?'

Chunni came running out of the workshop. 'They are ready, Pappaji.'

As she approached the doorway he held out his hand.

'First, give me the rest of the money from those unwanted leaflets. I assume you have sold them to the recycler by now, like I told you.'

Chunni shook her head, and her father's bloodshot eyes widened. Quickly, she continued.

'Not yet, Pappaji. I have had a better idea.' Chunni pulled a homemade fan out from behind her back. She opened it wide and began fanning herself with it. 'It is a fan,' she said.

'I can see that, girl. I am not stupid. Why are you showing it to me?'

'Because I made it from one of the leaflets. Each one is the perfect size and thickness to make a fan. And I have

172

collected a thousand lollipop sticks for the ends. There are even some old pots of bookbinding glue in the workshop. We have everything we need to make hundreds of them. The weather is unusually hot for this time of year. We can sell them in the market and make far more money than the recycler will pay us.'

Mr Kumar hesitated. He took the fan from Chunni and turned it around in his hands. It was perfectly folded, as he would have expected, and the gluing seemed straight and firm.

'Where did you learn to make this?' he asked.

'Amil showed me, the fan is his idea,' Chunni replied. The moment those words left her mouth Chunni regretted them.

Instantly, Mr Kumar flew into a rage. 'That boy! Who does he think he is to tell me how to run my business? And you, do you think you are a businessman now?'

'No, Pappaji, but . . .'

'Kumar and Sons does not make fans,' he roared. 'We are the oldest and most respected printing works in Bhopal. Now, for once, do as I tell you, and take the paper to the recyclers. And be sure to get a good price, otherwise we will all be eating cockroaches for dinner.' He ripped the fan in half and threw it back at her. 'I do not wish to hear another word about fans, do you hear?'

Chunni's face hardened, the protective unsmiling veil

which she had dared lift for a moment in anticipation of her father's approval fell back into place. She would do as she was told.

After setting out her father's breakfast, Chunni rejoined Amil in the workshop. Amil had heard the earlier commotion and had already loaded the cart. Together, they wheeled it silently out of the workshop and made their way through the noisy, bustling streets to the recyclers. Amil could see that Chunni was in no mood for cheering up. The last time he had tried, it had not worked. In fact, presenting her with the fan had turned into a disaster. So, they did not speak.

Mr Kumar was waiting for them outside the workshop when they returned. He held out his hand and Chunni dutifully dropped the recycling money into it.

'Is that all?' he demanded. Chunni promised him that it was. Mr Kumar's mouth tightened, as though he had just sucked on a lemon. 'Get inside. And you too,' he said, pushing Amil into the workshop. 'Perhaps, if neither of you has any food tonight, you will negotiate a better price in future.'

Halfway through the evening a bowl was pushed through the hatch in the workshop door. Amil approached it with suspicion. It was slightly larger than normal and bore no sign of Chunni's floury fingerprints. Instead, a dirty cloth was draped over it, concealing its contents. Amil crouched in front of the bowl and carefully peeled back the cloth. Then he fell back, sending the bowl tumbling. A dozen cockroaches spilled out over the floor and scattered in all directions. As he cried out he could hear Jalesh laughing outside.

'You had better enjoy eating them, paper-folder. I went to a lot of trouble catching them for you.'

Amil was no stranger to cockroaches. Even so, he retreated to his hammock, only returning to the workshop an hour later, when he heard his uncle calling to him. For once, to Amil's dismay, Uncle Ravi had arrived empty-handed and, although he was glad to see him, it was hard to listen to what he had to say when all he could hear was the rumbling of his own stomach. And his uncle had plenty to say. So much to say, in fact, that he did not have time even to sit down. Instead, as Amil sat on the floor listening to his stomach, his uncle paced up and down the workshop, stopping occasionally to wag a finger at Amil in order to emphasise a point. There had been more redundancies at the pesticide plant, he told him.

'Now I must look for the leaks, and tighten the nuts, *and* replace the valves, something for which I am not properly trained. The factory is turning to rust before our eyes, Amil. Our team used to check every valve once a week. Now we barely have time to check them once a month. There is so much to do that nobody knows where to start, so everyone is merely standing around doing nothing but watch the weeds grow. The general manager says that because no one is buying pesticide this year, the chemicals will remain in the storage tanks unused. But that is even more reason to keep the plant in tip-top condition. Instead, they are telling us to cut corners, so that the entire place is falling apart. I am doing my best, Amil. But I cannot follow their foolish orders for much longer. The whole situation is shaping up to be a disaster of epic proportions.'

At last, Amil spoke. 'What will become of my parents, Chachaji?'

The concern in his voice punctured his uncle's anger like a pinprick. He stopped pacing the room and squatted down in front of Amil.

'You must not worry,' he assured him, 'I am sending them money to buy seed and fertiliser for next year. They will thrive and prosper, you will see. Who knows, one day, instead of working at the pesticide plant you may decide to become a farmer yourself. Perhaps you will become one of our best customers, and I will have to start calling you "sir". How does that sound?'

Amil smiled. His uncle Ravi always made him feel safe. So did Sanjiv. After his uncle left, Amil climbed up to the attic and jumped into the hammock with the journal. His great-grandfather had not appeared from the rag pile in over a week, and Amil missed him. He turned to a new page. Almost immediately there was a sense of urgency in the handwriting, as though the long days of waiting had ended, and words could be scrawled only in fleeting moments.

'Please excuse my handwriting,' said a voice from the corner. 'Suddenly, I had work to do.'

'Where have you been?' asked Amil.

'Here, asleep,' Sanjiv replied. 'Waiting around is so tedious. During those long days, waiting for our attack to begin, I would often doze off. But Kush was not like me. He barely slept. He was like a lion waiting to fight, pacing up and down the trench as though it were a cage, unable to do anything except sharpen his claws. I have never seen a rifle so well-greased and ready for action as his, no bayonet blade so keen. There were days when I feared he might climb out of the trench and hurl himself alone at the enemy. Fortunately, two days before the attack the captain asked for volunteers to go to our company headquarters to collect the gas cylinders. The ground between us and the town was so churned up that no carriages could get through, he explained, so dozens of men would be needed to collect the cylinders and bring them back to the trench. Volunteers would leave under cover of darkness and return the following night with the cylinders. In between, they would be able to enjoy a day behind the lines, with the opportunity of a bath, a meal and a few hours' respite from the mud. As company runners, Deepak and Dev had to remain behind, but Kush raised his hand immediately.

'"Gujar here will come with me." He nudged me in the ribs. "You and me on the town for a day. What do you think of that?"

'So volunteered, Kush and I spent the day writing letters home for the other men, ready to deliver to the post office in town. Whilst some of them recounted their heroic adventures, others complained about our high casualty rates and the difference between our pay and that of our British counterparts, sentiments which, we warned them, might not get past the censors. We too, wrote letters home. I told Naisha that I was well, and in good spirits, and that she should not worry about me. *I am side by side with my best friends,* I told her, *and waiting for news.*

'That night as the light began to fade and with our kitbags bulging with post, we began the long muddy trudge back to the town, along what was left of the old farm tracks. The journey of three miles took us well over an hour. On arrival at the manor house which served as our HQ, we checked in with the officer in charge. Both of us were hoping that our incoming mail would be waiting for us, but we were told that it would not arrive at the post office until the following afternoon. I would have to wait another day to find out if I was yet a father. Having refilled our water bottles and picked up some provisions for the evening, all that remained for us to do was find somewhere to sleep. We were directed to a barn on the other side of the town. When we arrived, it took us some time to recognise it as the barn in which we had slept several months earlier. It remained standing, but the farmhouse next to it had not escaped the war. One entire wall had been destroyed, opening up the rooms inside to public gaze, like an open wound. The tree under which the old captain's horse had once been tethered had also been burned and broken beyond recognition, its shredded branches now like huge blackened fingers reaching for the sky.

'"It looks like it is surrendering," Kush said to me. "Clearly, it is not an Indian variety."

'We arrived at the same time as a column of men returning from another part of the front. Under the moonlight, they appeared to be marching in line. But, as they drew closer, I could see that their arms were not swinging by their sides, neither were their heads held straight. Instead, with a medical orderly leading the way, the hand of each man rested on the shoulder of the man in front, his eyes bandaged, head bowed, coughing and choking as his body tried to expel the gas that had invaded his lungs. Unlike other walking wounded I had seen, these men shuffled as well as they could in step, as though on parade. I knew from my time in Brighton that without the sound of each other's feet keeping each man safely anchored to the fellow in front, the line would be broken, and they would be lost. As they passed us, one of the soldiers fell out of step and lost his grip on the man in front. He in turn stopped, and soon the entire column had come to a standstill. I led the errant soldier back into line, returning his blistered hand to the shoulder of the man in front.

' "When did the enemy attack you?" I asked.

' "They did not attack us," he rasped, as though an invisible hand was gripping his throat. "We attacked them."

'As the column snaked into the barn, Kush and I decided not to follow the men inside. The night was crisp but not frosty, the sky clear and bright under a full moon. The ruins of a small brick outhouse a few yards from the barn gave us some shelter from the wind, and part of the stone floor remained intact, offering us a dry base on which to sleep. Despite the rain of the previous week the charred remains of the tree provided us with enough dry wood to make a small campfire. We made ourselves comfortable in our temporary accommodation. As the moon moved across the sky, Kush and I shared a ration of biscuits, whilst watching the endless stream of tiny glowing embers rising from our fire, like souls from a funeral pyre.

' "There are so many dead," he said. He threw a lump

of wood on to the fire, sending another thousand souls flickering into the night sky. "This war is not what I imagined it to be. Death is manufactured here, and we are nothing more than its raw ingredients, mined from our lands, diced up, melted down, and poured into the mud. There is no glory in that. I think I am beginning to understand the poems that Captain Bradbury read to us." He stared into the fire, shaking his head. "I should not have dragged you and my brothers here." But I told him he was wrong. From my pocket, I pulled out a handful of cigarette cards that I had collected to send home to Mani. I held them up to him.

'"We all need to be able to look these men in the eye if ever we should meet them," I told him. "Without honour we would shrink under their gaze, like a goat standing before a lion. Your brothers and I have as much right as you to earn their respect, and to fight for the great prize of independence that has been promised to our country. Remember, we are here for our future sons and daughters, Kush, not the British. That is where the glory lies."

'Kush prodded the fire with a stick. "I just want to fight," he said.

'Despite a constant rumbling in the distance, we slept soundly that night. I awoke just as the sun was rising, casting an orange glow over the land to match the dying embers of the fire.'

As his great-grandfather spoke, Amil realised that the same orange glow appeared to be lighting the pages of his journal. His torch was dying too. He tapped the side of it, hoping it might brighten. Instead, the light dimmed even more.

'It is a shame you cannot simply throw some wood on it,' Sanjiv observed. 'That morning, a few twigs were enough to bring our fire back to life. Once I had replenished it, I sat with my back against the wall, staring at the tree as its silhouette surrendered to the sunrise. A solitary leaf clung on to what remained of its branches, the last of its fellows to meet its fate. Soon, it too would fall. And I knew precisely where. Had the wind chosen that moment to separate if it from the tree I could see every twist and turn, every swoop and swivel of its descent, leading inevitably to a watery grave in the puddle several yards from where it hung. I prodded the fire once more, then watched the smoke billow upwards, knowing how each waft and curl would unfold, as easily as one might predict the words of a much-loved song. The movement of the wind was no mystery to me. The gods had given me a gift; I was sure of it. The real mystery to me was why.

'When Kush awoke, we warmed ourselves against the fire, sharing another ration of biscuits. The prospect of a proper meal at our headquarters and the chance to spend the day exploring the town cheered us, and we were in a jovial mood. As we set about packing our things, we discussed our task. The gas cylinder would weigh the same as three men, and would be suspended beneath a pole carried between us. We realised that to avoid sinking into the mud on our return, we would need to take a longer route back to our trench, over more solid ground. Determined to make the most of our day, we doused the fire without further ado. Then we set off, pausing only to wave to the farmer's daughter, who was crossing the courtyard taking water to the men.

'"They say that carrying a cylinder is like carrying a tiger after a hunt. Except that it is still deadly," Kush said, as we broke into our stride.

'"I imagine you know all about tigers," I told him.

'"Why is that?" he asked.

'"Because you look as though you have been mauled a few times," I said.

'Kush pretended to be insulted – for in truth he knew himself to be a handsome fellow – and he chased me down the track. After a few yards I turned, readying myself for whatever playful punishment Kush was about to administer for my insolence. Instead, the look in his eyes was as fierce as I had ever seen it. For a split second, I feared he was about to sink his teeth into my throat. I cried out as he launched himself at me, hands splayed like claws, sending us both headlong over a low hedge into the ditch on the other side. Then there was a *crump*, a sound so dense and heavy that I could feel the earth tremble beneath me. Kush lay on top of me, pressing me into the mud as the shell ripped the earth open less than a hundred yards away from us, sending a mountain of mud and debris into the air, as if it had erupted from a volcano. We lay motionless as it rained down around us, and I could feel Kush's body jolt as pieces of earth and wood and stone landed on him. Only when the last clod of earth had fallen did he release his grip on me. When we emerged from the ditch, the wall we had slept beside was no longer there, neither was the barn, nor the men who had bedded down in it. There was nothing but a giant steaming hole in the ground, and the sound of the farmer's wife screaming for her daughter.

'"You see," Kush said, stabbing a finger at the crater, "we are not soldiers. We are no more than ants trampled under a giant mechanical boot. And that is its damn footprint!"

'We ran back to help as best we could, leaving only once medics and stretcher bearers had arrived, not that there was much they could do. As we departed, Kush strode out in front of me, keen to get away from the farm now that our duty there was done. The back of his coat was torn and peppered with small explosions of mud, as though it had been used for target practice. He had shielded me from a barrage of debris, with little more than a grunt

184

each time a chunk of it landed on top of him. It had always been so. Even though we were the same age, he had always protected me like a younger brother. Whilst Deepak and Dev looked after each other and Mani was under the wing of his parents, I was the one he had protected on the streets of Bhopal and, twice now, in France. "You would do the same for me," he would say. But I never had. Perhaps I would never be more than a goat after all, for ever riding on the back of this brave and benevolent lion. But that is not how true friendship should be. And it was not my wish.

'I caught up with him and brushed the dirt from his back as best I could, before falling into step beside him. We no longer had an appetite for sightseeing, and decided instead to go to the post office to collect our company mail, and then back to our headquarters. As we arrived there, we passed a line of men queuing to collect gas cylinders from a solid-looking stone outbuilding in its grounds, chosen no doubt to protect its contents from anything other than a direct hit from the enemy. As two men left bearing a cylinder on the pole between them, another two entered to collect their cargo, emerging fully-laden shortly afterwards to find a resting place before their departure.

'"I would rather not carry one of those on an empty stomach," Kush remarked. So we headed straight for the canteen. A few minutes later, in the shelter of a barn, with a meal in front of us and bales of hay at our backs, we sifted through the mail sack. There was one letter addressed to Kush and his brothers, and one to me from my wife, both written in Old Mr Kumar's distinctive hand, as Naisha could not write for herself. Kush ripped open his letter and devoured its contents as eagerly as the food on his plate.

'"All is well," he told me, stuffing the letter into the pocket of his uniform. Then he grinned. "Your turn," he said, impatiently. "Naisha has some good news for you." I took a deep breath and opened the letter. Then, my heart leaped.'

Suddenly, Amil's torch flickered out. He shook it, momentarily bringing it back to life.

'Pardada, *Pardada*. What did she say in the letter?'

'Have you not guessed?' his great-grandfather replied. 'She said I had a son.'

18
Mrs Sharma's Fan

With the battery of his torch flat, Amil was tempted to continue reading Sanjiv's journal during daylight. But, over the next few days Chunni stayed by his side, and insisted that he accompany her as she visited every customer of Kumar and Sons, past and present.

'My father is so angry,' she explained. 'He knows the fan was a good idea, but he cannot bear the thought that it was yours. I should never have told him. Now you will not be safe until we can drum up some ordinary paper-folding work that he can call his own.'

So, day after day, Amil waited outside a succession of printworks whilst Chunni ventured inside, to be greeted by sympathetic shaking of heads, but no paper-folding work. Occasionally, she would emerge with a bag of rags or paper offcuts which they would sell on their way home, and once or twice she found a tourist willing to lose a rupee or two betting on the flight of a feather. But each time, even though he knew that restoring his family name was an honourable objective, he felt that parting strangers from their money was not the right way to achieve it. Like Sanjiv, he felt that he had been given his gift for a purpose. Also, like Sanjiv, he did not yet know what that purpose was.

Each day, as they returned from the day's excursion, Amil would take the cart into the workshop, whilst Chunni would head into the house to prepare dinner for Jalesh and her father. On the Thursday of that week, she returned to find her father waiting for her in the doorway. He grabbed her arm and dragged her inside, slamming the door shut behind him.

'Guess who I saw in the market today,' he said.

'I do not know, Pap—'

'Mrs Sharma, from the chicken shop,' he spat, 'and do you know what she was doing?' Chunni backed against the wall, shaking her head. 'She was fanning herself! With a fan made out of a pesticide leaflet! You have been selling them behind my back! Where is the money?'

He raised his hand to strike her just as Jalesh appeared in the doorway. 'I have looked everywhere, even under her mattress. There is nothing there except an old shopping bag.'

'I have not been selling fans, Pappaji. I took the leaflets to the recycler as you instructed.'

'Then how did Mrs Sharma come to be using the fan? Did she sneak into the workshop and make it herself? Do you think I am stupid?'

'Amil made a fan for me weeks ago. I gave it to Mrs Sharma because she had heatstroke. I did not make any more of them. I took the leaflets to the recyclers; you can ask them. They will even tell you how much they paid me. I gave you every rupee.'

Mr Kumar lowered his hand. He and Jalesh had searched the house from top to bottom. There was no sign of any money. Even worse for Mr Kumar, the missing cigarette card had not turned up. Not that Jalesh had expected them to find it. Even though his father always told him that it was such a rare and valuable specimen that he would never have thrown it away by mistake, Jalesh had searched the house enough times to know that it was not there. As a result, watching his father scrabbling around on all fours in search of it, had become increasingly enjoyable.

Mr Kumar wagged his finger in Chunni's face, his lips trembling in search of words that might justify his anger. But none came, and after a few seconds he turned his back on her and stormed out of the house. Chunni breathed a long heavy sigh. Then she started to walk towards the doorway. But Jalesh reached it before her, stretching his arm across it to bar her way.

'I know what you are doing,' he said. 'You may fool our idiot father, but not me.'

Chunni said nothing.

'You are protecting that Gujar boy again; do you think

189

I have not noticed? *He* is the one who has been stealing our paper to make fans. You did not give that fan to Mrs Sharma. The paper-folder has been selling them. He is a thief as well as a lowly coward!' Jalesh turned abruptly and ran across the road. Amil was in the attic, gazing out of the skylight when he burst through the hatch. 'All very cosy,' Jalesh said, looking at the hammock. His eyes scanned the room, looking for clues. They did not need to look far. On a shelf he found some old pots of glue, and a couple of lollipop sticks. All the evidence he needed. He grabbed Amil's arm and dragged him off the trunk. Amil landed on the floorboards with a heavy thud. 'Is the money in here?' Jalesh said, throwing open the lid. He reached into the kitbag and pulled out Sanjiv's journal, which he sent spinning across the floor. Then he pulled out Sanjiv's gas mask. As with the journal, the two round windows in the side of the strange white sack failed to arouse even a shred of curiosity in him. All Jalesh noticed was the weight and feel of the bundle of coins inside it. He upturned the mask and the bag of money fell out, followed by a handful of loose rupees. 'You filthy thief! You have been making fans with our paper and selling them.'

Just in time, Chunni's head appeared through the hatch. 'No, he has not. You can check yourself at the recycling station. All of it was sold.'

'Then he has stolen this money from our father. He has

been sneaking into the house and stealing it whilst we slept. There can be no other explanation.' Jalesh grabbed Amil by his hair. 'My father will give you the beating of your life for this. That is after I have finished with you.' Jalesh pulled back his fist, and Amil closed his eyes.

'He won it!'

Jalesh hesitated. He pushed Amil against the wall, pinning him there as he turned to Chunni. She climbed into the room.

'He did not steal it. He won it,' she said. 'Every rupee. I was going to use it to buy back Pappa's old printing press.'

Jalesh tightened his grip on Amil. 'I do not believe you,' he snarled. 'He could not have won it. He is a Gujar. He is useless at everything.'

Chunni put a hand on her brother's arm.

'We will show you, won't we, Amil?'

Amil opened his eyes and nodded. He had no choice.

'I have to show you outside,' he said, his voice trembling. Jalesh let him go, then bent down to scoop up the money. He stuffed it into his pockets until they bulged like two puffed-out cheeks. Then he led the way down the steps to the workshop, and out into the street. There, leaning against the workshop door with his arms crossed, he signalled for the demonstration to begin.

'This had better be good,' he said. From her pocket, Chunni took out a small white feather and handed it to

Amil. 'Ha! A white feather,' Jalesh mocked. 'That is what they give to cowards. But I expect Gujar knows that already, I am sure that his family has received hundreds of them.'

Despite the difference in size between him and Jalesh, Amil could feel a rage building inside him. A glance from Chunni steadied him.

Then she turned to Jalesh. 'Where would you like him to throw it?'

Jalesh was so accustomed to lying that it took him several hours to believe the evidence of his own eyes. He made Amil throw feathers up drainpipes, into the baskets of passing bicycles and the gaping mouths of panting dogs.

'Send it around that lamppost and back into your hand,' he commanded. 'Make it land on the nose of that old woman to make her sneeze. Make it hover. Make it spin. Throw two feathers at once.'

Amil accomplished each feat flawlessly until, by the end of the afternoon, Jalesh was convinced that Chunni had given him the truth. And much more. She had given him a way out of school, a way out of work, even the chance to get away from Bhopal and his father. For Jalesh was in no doubt that Amil was invincible. A bet on Amil was a bet won. Better still, apart from a handful of tourists – most of them long gone – few people knew of Amil's gift. Everyone else in Bhopal would bet against him.

For who would bet on the impossible? Using the money that rightfully belonged to the Kumar family, and so to him, Jalesh would take their bets. He would take on every gambler in Bhopal and win a fortune. But he would need help from someone who could gather them together. Someone who could arrange the biggest bet the city had ever seen. He tapped one of his bulging pockets, turning his head between Amil and Chunni to ensure that both of them understood clearly.

'This is mine now,' he told them. 'And if either of you mentions it to my father, I shall tell him that I have been saving up to buy back his old printing press, and that you stole it from me. In a thousand years he will not believe either of you. I am the only one he trusts.'

Chunni looked bereft.

'Go inside and do some cooking, like you are supposed to,' Jalesh told her, 'Amil and I have some business to attend to.' Then, he took Amil by the arm and led him down the street. 'Your little party trick belongs to me now,' he said.

19

The Gambler

Even though Hari Laghari was closer to his father's age than his own, Jalesh looked up to him like an older brother. He was everything that Jalesh aspired to be and was not: respected, feared, successful. Unlike Jalesh, who strutted around looking the part, Hari achieved all of this from behind a dishevelled and absent-minded facade. He kept his sharp piercing eyes shielded from view behind a pair of sunglasses which rested permanently on his long beaky nose. His strong sinewy limbs lay concealed, ready for action underneath a collection of baggy, badly buttoned-up shirts, whilst, like a magician's sleight of hand, his head of muddled, unkempt hair diverted attention from the razor-sharp mind lurking beneath it. Hari Laghari was a man to underestimate at one's peril. Above all though, like Amil, he possessed a rare, albeit very different, gift. Whereas Amil could read the wind, Hari could read the eyes of any person foolish enough to set foot in his gambling den. Just by glancing into them he could tell whether a person was being truthful, or lying, or bluffing.

Looking deeper, he could see how desperate they were to win, how much they would bet, and what risks they would take. Deeper still, and those eyes would reveal what lay behind them, be it cruelty or stupidity or, in the case of Jalesh, both. Gambling was the perfect vocation for his talent, and the gambling house – which he had inherited from his father – the perfect location for it. Situated in the Old City, it lay midway between the slums to the east, and the more affluent area to the west. Around the assortment of tables in the large basement room, cockfights were arranged, games of chance and poker played. On to these tables the poor from the slums would plant their last remaining rupees – like grains of hope scraped from the linings of their pockets – and will them to grow into fortunes. Fuelled by the cheap alcohol that Hari supplied to anyone holding a hand of cards, the better-off would soon find themselves waging a month's pay on a hunch, whilst any tourist foolish enough to venture inside – even to ask for directions – would emerge into the daylight picked clean like a chicken carcass.

With Amil clasped to his side, Jalesh walked into the basement. Hari Laghari was alone, counting money at one of his tables.

'Hari, I have a business proposition for you which you cannot afford to miss,' Jalesh announced confidently.

Hari peered over the top of his glasses. One look into

the eyes of his visitor told him that, for once, Jalesh was not bluffing. He stood up and locked the door behind them, before dropping the key into the pocket of his shirt.

'You can let the boy go, now,' he said.

Jalesh released his grip and Amil stepped away, rubbing his arm. Looking around him, he noticed that unlike other establishments he had visited with Chunni, the room was not adorned with posters or photographs or any kinds of religious symbols or decoration. Instead, the walls of the gambling den were lined with the feathers of numerous cockerels – many of them ruffled and stained with blood that had dried brown with age. Each feather was pressed beneath a glass frame alongside an old cigarette card, bearing the name of the Indian war hero after whom its original owner was named. Hari noticed Amil's eyes scanning the wall, his lips moving almost imperceptibly as he read the names. Some of them Amil recognised from Sanjiv's journal – names of Indian soldiers famed for their gallantry, who had inspired Sanjiv and his friends in the trenches.

'This is Kulbir Thapa V.C.,' Hari said, straightening one of the frames. 'He dodged a thousand bullets to carry injured comrades to safety in front of enemy guns – a feat of such bravery that the king of England presented a gallantry medal to him in person. Every fine warrior deserves a memorial, do you not agree? Over the years, every bird in my service has been named after an Indian warrior, and has carried the same gallant fighting spirit into the cockfighting ring.'

Amil's attention was drawn to the centre of the collection. There, in pride of place, was a brown-speckled feather, the only feather with a blank space alongside it where a cigarette card should have been. Hari tapped the glass with a long fingernail which, Amil was alarmed to notice, was cut to a point like the talon of a fighting cockerel.

'And this is Darwan Singh Negi V.C., named after a truly valiant soldier,' he explained. 'He was my most successful and profitable bird, winner of eleven glorious victories before falling under the claw of a young upstart twice his size. Would you believe the bird that beat him was named after an English footballer?' Hari shook his head. 'There used to be honour and dignity in the cockfighting business. Now all the birds are named after western popstars or preening footballers. That is not right. These animals fight to the death; they deserve respect.' Hari turned to Jalesh. 'Has your father found the missing card yet?'

Jalesh laughed. 'No, but he still looks for it, the idiot. At least once a week he says to me, "Jalesh, have you seen the cigarette card of Darwan Singh Negi?" He thinks you will pay a handsome price to complete the set.'

Hari turned to Amil. 'Jalesh's father used to be one of this establishment's best customers,' he explained, 'by all accounts a man truly dedicated to his vice. He presented these cards to my father over twenty years ago to pay off a gambling debt. Or at least a small part of it. Had he not lost one of the cards – belonging to this fellow here, Darwan Singh Negi – the set would have been complete, and he would not have had to sell his printing press to pay off the rest. If he finds it now I may give him a few rupees for it, but I have grown used to the blank space. Besides, even if I had the full set, times have changed. There is no longer a market for such collections.'

'I am not surprised,' Jalesh sneered, 'who cares about some old soldiers from the Second World War?'

'First World War,' Amil corrected him, quietly. Jalesh looked down at him and frowned, but Hari was impressed.

'Very good. Clearly, you are vastly more knowledgeable than your friend here,' he observed. Amil winced. Jalesh would make him pay for that comment. 'Let us hope that his business proposition is better than his knowledge of history,' Hari continued, turning to Jalesh. 'So, what is it that you propose?'

Jalesh gripped Amil's arm rather harder than was necessary and pulled him to his side.

'This Gujar boy has a very remarkable talent,' he explained. 'He can tell which way the wind blows.'

Hari licked his forefinger and held it aloft.

'Any fool can do that,' he said.

'Not like him,' said Jalesh, 'he can *see* the path of the wind. He knows precisely where it is going even before it gets there. This boy –' he paused for effect – 'can throw a feather in a hurricane and get it to land wherever he likes.'

Hari's eyes widened.

'The wind outside is quite strong,' Jalesh continued, 'we will be happy to give you a demonstration.'

Hari crouched down in front of Amil and pushed his sunglasses up on to his forehead. Without warning he clamped Amil's head between his hands, holding it tight so that he could look into his eyes. With the points of his thumbnails pressed gently, but menacingly, below Amil's eyes, Hari tilted his head slowly from side to side as though he were peering behind them, seeking out anything that might be hidden from view.

'Is what Jalesh says true? A hurricane?' he asked.

Amil tried to nod. 'P-probably. Although I am not sure . . . about a tornado.' Hari released his grip and walked over to one of the tables. On it stood a large electric fan. 'Can you demonstrate using this?' he asked. Amil nodded again.

'Then you may show me in here,' Hari told him. He flipped a switch and the fan blades hummed into motion.

Jalesh removed a small chicken feather from his pocket and handed it to Amil.

'Where would you like me to throw it?' Amil asked.

Hari sat at the table and placed his hand in front of the fan.

'Here,' he said. Jalesh's face dropped, but Amil did not seem at all concerned. Already, he could feel the fan pushing the air around the basement, weaving a circuit around the chairs and tables and every other obstacle in its path. He removed his shirt and flexed his fingers. Then he walked around the room, pausing occasionally to crouch down, or stand on a chair, or close his eyes to feel the minor ripples in air flow caused by the slightest movement of Hari's hand, or Jalesh's nervous fidgeting.

Finally, he was ready. Reaching up on his toes from a table at the far end of the room, he released the feather an inch below the ceiling. It bumped along it in a straight line, tickling the plasterwork until it reached the far wall. There, it hovered for a moment, like an eagle lining up its prey, before drifting down at a steep angle across the face of the fan. The next thing Hari knew, the feather had become wedged between two of his fingers.

'You did not say land the feather *on top* of your hand,' Amil explained, 'that would have been more difficult.'

Hari opened his fingers, and the feather floated on its

way. For the first time in his career, his eyes betrayed the delight of being dealt an unbeatable hand.

'Well! I have seen a few feathers fly in my time, but never like that.' He stood up and removed the feather of Darwan Singh Negi from its frame. He handed it to Amil, and turned the fan on to its maximum setting. 'Show me again,' he said.

Half an hour later, Hari Laghari slumped back in his chair, digesting the magic he had just witnessed repeated a dozen times. He had only one more question. He turned to Jalesh, studying his eyes for any trace of uncertainty.

'Can the boy be trusted not to let us down?' he asked him.

Jalesh smiled. The answer to that was easy. Everything he had ever been told about the Gujar family confirmed it. As sure as the sun rose and fell each day, this, to Jalesh Kumar, was the absolute, unquestionable truth.

'Completely. The boy comes from a long line of gutless cowards. In a thousand lifetimes he would not dare to double-cross us.' To emphasise the threat his hand moved to the back of Amil's neck. He squeezed until Amil yelped with pain and buckled at the knees.

Hari raised his hand.

'Enough! One thing I have learned arranging cockfights is that it is not a good idea to wring a chicken's neck until *after* it has performed. And even then, only if it loses.' He crouched down to Amil. 'As you are such an expert, I am sure you know what punishment befell traitors during the First World War?' Amil shook his head, for Sanjiv had never spoken of it. Hari brought his lips to Amil's ear. 'Execution,' he whispered. 'The same as for cowardice.'

Despite the muggy heat being pushed around the room by the fan, Amil shivered. Hari jumped to his feet and clapped his hands together. 'Good. Now that we all understand each other, we can get down to business!' he said.

And so it was agreed, that a special, once-in-a-lifetime bet would take place in the local square on the following Sunday. On that day, few people would be working and most of the shops would be closed. What better way for the citizens of Bhopal to end the weekend than with one last throw of the dice – or in this case, feather – before returning to the drudgery of work the following morning. Hari was confident that the moment he announced what he would call the 'Bet of the Century', word would spread like wildfire around the gambling dens of Bhopal. Apart from Jalesh's father – who had long ago been banned from all of them – every gambler in the city would hear of it. Then, on Sunday, they would flock to the square, each to place a bet that they believed they could not lose. But lose it they would. As Jalesh sat with Hari discussing the arrangements, he felt for the first time in his life, that he was on the winning side. Not only was he in partnership with the feared and revered Hari Laghari but, in return for providing the services of Amil, his new partner had agreed to lend him a thousand rupees to increase his stake. Between the two of them they would cover all bets placed against the boy, knowing beyond any shadow of doubt that every rupee would end up in their pockets. After all, they had seen Amil perform his remarkable trick faultlessly, time after time after time. What could possibly go wrong?

20
A Warning

Amil returned from the gambling den of Hari Laghari feeling nothing but dread for his starring role in the forthcoming so-called 'Bet of the Century'. The gift given to him by his great-grandfather had been stolen from him just as surely as Chunni's life savings had been stolen from their hiding place. His gift had felt as much a part of him as the thoughts in his head and the sound of his voice, and yet he was no longer master of it. Instead, he felt as though a parasite had entered his body and begun to control him. The thought of it made him feel sick, as though his body wanted to flush it out on to the floor of the workshop. He climbed into one of the plastic chairs and sat cradling his knees. As Chunni pushed his evening meal through the hatch he did not stir. He did not notice the floury smile she had drawn on the side of the bowl to uplift his spirits. Instead, he continued to stare blankly at the door, dreaming of escape, even though he knew he could not.

Suddenly, two angry voices barged into his dream from the street outside. They belonged to Mr Kumar and his uncle Ravi, who was not due to visit him for several days. At least, that was according to Mr Kumar, whose bitter protestations Amil could hear clearly on the other side of the door. Then the shouting stopped, and the door swung open. His uncle entered the workshop, lopsided under the weight of a bulging holdall slung over one shoulder. Amil noticed also that, for once, he was not wearing his overalls or his safety helmet.

'Chachaji!' Amil rushed forwards and threw his arms around his uncle, almost knocking him over. 'Have you come to take me away?'

Uncle Ravi shook his head.

'You cannot leave here, Amil. You know that.' He prised Amil away from him, then crouched down to clasp him by the shoulders, as though he were a delicate vase in danger of falling. He took a deep breath. 'I have come to tell you that I am leaving Bhopal with your auntie Maya and the girls. We are going to join your mother and father and the rest of your family in the countryside.'

Amil's mouth dropped open, but no words came out. So his uncle continued.

'The farmers have not been buying pesticide, like I told you, so the plant has stopped making it. It is like a ghost town there now. Even the safety systems have been shut down, much to my disgust. I have told them that they are gambling with the lives of every person in Bhopal, because the poisonous chemicals are still there, sitting like timebombs in those giant tanks. But no one will listen to me. To them I am merely a humble foot soldier, you see. Bottom of the heap. They will listen only to those of higher rank. That is why, when the general manager ordered his officers to save money, the safety officer fired me and my colleagues without a thought for the consequences. I told him in no uncertain terms that he should be concerned with saving lives, not money. And do you know what he said?' Amil shook his head wearily. '"I am only following orders." I will not tell you what I said to that, but I am not expecting to receive a leaving present from him.

'So . . . from tomorrow, leaks will no longer be searched for, nuts and bolts will no longer be tightened, and valves will no longer be replaced. And all the time, the chemicals will continue to eat away at the insides of their tanks, constantly searching for ways to escape their confinement. As I have no doubt that, one day, they will. Because one day someone will make a terrible mistake, or one of the valves will finally fall apart. When that happens, assuming they have not turned it off to save more money, the siren will sound. The moment you hear it –' he gripped Amil's shoulders tighter and made sure he was looking into his eyes – 'you must run like the wind, like I told you. Get as far away from here as you can. Do you understand?'

Amil nodded. Uncle Ravi let go of him and unzipped

his bag. He took out a box about the size and weight of a house brick, and handed it to him. 'At least one of us can have a leaving present,' he said. 'By the time that box is empty, your time here will be over, and you will be free again.'

Then he stood up, vigorously ruffling his hair as though he were trying to shake out an army of nits. 'I cannot get rid of the imprint of that damn helmet,' he muttered.

Finally, he heaved his holdall back on to his shoulder.

'One day, you will return to us, Amil. And you will be happy. I promise.'

Still Amil did not speak. Tears welled up in his eyes. First his mother and father, his brothers and grandparents. And now, his beloved chachaji. All gone. He looked down at the box, wondering what was inside. Slowly, as though it might contain some fresh unforeseen horror, he lifted the lid. Tears cascaded down his cheeks as he gazed at the batteries packed tightly inside, like rows of soldiers standing to attention. By the time he looked up again, his uncle was gone.

21

Ripples in the Sky

A mil and Chunni saw little of each other over the following two days. With Sunday approaching, Jalesh forced Amil to practise throwing feathers from dawn to dusk. After all, Jalesh's future was at stake. If the bet went well, he would no longer even have to pretend to go to school. He would have enough money to do whatever he liked. He could even take Amil away and repeat the bet in other cities.

They practised in the square, so that Amil could familiarise himself with the prevailing air flows circulating around it, and the obstacles that might have a bearing on them on the day. Jalesh was also keen to avoid his father. Although he knew that having been banned from every gambling establishment in Bhopal, he was unlikely even to hear of the event, Jalesh had chosen a square devoid of tea houses, or anything else that might attract his father on a Sunday. It was he who had discovered gold. Not his father. As he sat on a low wall watching Amil throw feathers into an old tin can placed on a nearby window ledge, he imagined himself as a great showman: rich, successful, respected. He was the one with the talent, the one who made it all happen, like the trainer of a performing animal.

For his part, Amil performed his tasks perfectly, but with no satisfaction or delight in the use of his ability. He and the wind had been subjugated to the whims of his tormentor, and for whatever purpose he had inherited his gift, it certainly was not this. He felt that not just he, but the eternal, majestic force of Vayu, God of the Wind, was being humbled and ridiculed, made to perform for an unworthy purpose, like a shackled elephant forced to do headstands for the amusement of the crowd.

Chunni too went about her daily chores with a blankness in her eyes. It was true that Amil had never seen them sparkle, but the piercing gaze with which she normally looked at everything around her, assessing its value and potential to put food on the table, was gone now too. Passing Chunni on her way back from Mr Sharma's chicken shop, Amil enquired after the health of Mrs Sharma.

'She is fully recovered,' Chunni replied, 'but Mr Sharma says that when she returned from the market yesterday she was carried off by a crocodile, so there were no plucked chickens. I gave him ten rupees anyway. What is the point of saving money if it will always be stolen from me?'

'I am sorry,' Amil replied, his eyes filling up with tears. He knew that Chunni had always saved him: from her father, from Jalesh, even from the security guard at the pesticide plant. And yet, when she had needed him, he had let her down. 'I should have hidden your money somewhere else,' he said to her, miserably. 'The trunk was a stupid place. It even *looks* like a treasure chest.' Chunni's expression did not change, neither to a scowl of anger at Amil's admission, nor to a sympathetic smile. She simply pressed her lips together and shook her head gently.

'It is not your fault,' she said.

Amil did not venture into the attic until the night before the big bet in the square. When he did, he stood over the pile of rags in the corner staring silently at them with his fists clenched. He did not call out for his great-grandfather. Instead, after several minutes, he went in search of the journal which Jalesh had sent spinning into the far corner of the room. Having retrieved it, he dusted it off and climbed into the hammock. For a few moments he held the book tight against his chest, afraid that if he opened it the pages might reveal that Sanjiv had, indeed, been a coward, and that he was responsible for everything bad that had happened to Amil since his tenth birthday. Despite the rage which had been bubbling up inside him for several days, he did not want to be angry with his great-grandfather, especially now that his uncle Ravi had gone. More than anything he did not wish to become like Mr Kumar and

Jalesh, for ever blaming someone else for their misfortunes. And yet he needed to know what had happened all those years ago. So, finally, he opened the journal, feeling the air move as he flicked through the pages. Eventually, he came to a drawing of a bird. As he was looking at it, Sanjiv's head appeared out of the rag pile.

'It is a heron,' he said, rubbing his eyes. 'I drew it from memory, of course. There were no birds where we were. Every tree, every hedge, every bush in which they might alight or set up home, had been blasted out of existence. I drew it the day after Kush and I arrived back in the trench with the gas cylinder. The journey had taken us most of the night. And the mud! We kept to the old farm tracks, but still encountered enough of it to sink a battleship. Even though the news of my son made me feel as though I could fly, the mud managed to suck us down to our knees several times, so that the cylinder looked like a bottle floating in a thick black sea. We and the rest of the volunteers barely made it back by daybreak.

'The following day, those of us who had carried the cylinders through the night were given light duties and told to rest before the forthcoming battle. I cleaned my rifle, then strung the old captain's hammock across the entrance to an abandoned communications trench leading off our own. Once I had settled myself into it, I wrote to Naisha. I told her that I had blown a kiss into the wind, and that if she poked my son's head out of the attic skylight, it should arrive on his forehead shortly after reading my letter.' Sanjiv chuckled. 'I was joking, of course. We are not *that* clever, Amil. Having tucked the letter safely into my pocket, I lay back with my hands behind my head to rest. That day the sky was filled with hundreds of tiny clouds, which the captain had told me once were called cirrocumulus. They looked like ripples on the surface of a giant blue ocean – at least, as I imagined a bird in flight might see them. For some reason I took out my journal and drew a heron, perhaps because often I had watched them fly over the Upper Lake, using the wind to turn and glide, and help them get where they wanted to be.'

'Did you ever wonder whether you should be using the wind for some special purpose?' asked Amil.

'You mean apart from flying kites?' said Sanjiv.

Amil nodded. 'I do not know why I have been given my gift. I thought I knew. Mr Kumar said that for a million rupees I could pay back our family debt. But Jalesh will take everything I have now. So, what is the point of being able to predict the wind if I am powerless to use it?'

'I asked myself the same question many times,' Sanjiv replied, 'and I was about to find out the answer. I had put the journal away and was lying in the hammock, just as you are now, staring up at the sea of ripples above me. I dug out the lucky stone from beneath my uniform and stared through the hole in it, blanking out everything around me: voices, smells, the mud. I imagined that I was a heron flying over Upper Lake, looking down on the water as though, somewhere just beneath the foam-tipped ripples on its surface, there lay the answer. And then something very strange happened. Everything around me started to turn upside down, as though we were all living inside a giant ball that was rolling over. The whole world went topsy-turvy. Suddenly, instead of looking up at the clouds, I found myself falling through the air *towards* them. And I was not alone. Every soldier and his kit, every ammunition box, every spent cartridge, everything that was not fixed to the ground, fell with me through the air, leaving nothing on the muddied earth behind us but the scars of our trenches. And as we fell, before our eyes the sky became a beautiful turquoise sea.

Suddenly, with a mighty crash, we were under the water. As the sea consumed us, everything we wore and everything we carried was instantly stripped away. I spied my greatcoat nearby and reached for it to cover my nakedness. But the two collar buttons flashed at me and I realised that they were now the eyes of a huge grey flatfish. As my coat glided away, my bayonet turned into a silver eel, and around me a million rifle bullets spilled out of their ammunition boxes and turned into vast shoals of glinting goldfish. Below me, hundreds of grenades hit the ocean floor and exploded like huge blooming flowers to cover the seabed in life and colour. As I swam, my fingers and toes fused together, and my skin became a shining rainbow. Soon, we were no longer soldiers, we were simply fish, devoid of race, religion, caste, or nationality. Then, suddenly, it grew dark, as scores of gas cylinders floating slowly towards their journey's end cast menacing shadows over us. One by one, as they hit the seabed, they exploded, sending up huge swirling clouds of sand and foam which tossed us around like specks of dust in the wind. Then all was still. But not for long.

'From the murky waters, a huge tentacle reached into our midst and wrapped itself around the tailfin of one of my comrades. As it dragged him into the gloom another tentacle emerged, then dozens more, reaching in from every direction to gather their prey. When they had stopped feasting on us, the sand settled, and the water became clear. Only then did we see the monsters that had followed us into the water. Around and above what remained of us, a hundred giant squid, their razor-sharp beaks still dripping with the flesh of our comrades, circled slowly to prevent our escape.

'A sergeant-major fish swam over to us, his rank emblazoned on his sides in thick black stripes.

'"They will attack again soon," he said, a line of bubbles rising from his mouth. "We are too small in number to defend ourselves. Someone must go for help."

' "I will go," I said.

'The sergeant-major fish laughed. "You are a brave little fish, but Deepak and Dev are the fastest. Only they can outswim those great lumbering monsters."

' "But I am the fiercest," said Kush. "If any of those tentacles comes near me, I will bite it in half. Let me go."

' "In that case, the three of you shall set off together," said the sergeant-major fish. "And do not think to follow your friends, Sanjiv Gujar. That is an order."

'As my friends prepared to leave, I felt the water moving around me, making patterns across my scales as if it were talking to me in a language that only I could understand. Suddenly, I knew that my scales could read the ebbs and flows of the ocean, and that the water would guide me to safety. But I dared not disobey an order. So, I did nothing. Instead, I watched my three best friends set off to their doom.

'Sure enough, Deepak was not fast enough to evade the huge tentacles that reached out for him. I heard no beguiling words come from his mouth to trick his captor into releasing him, only his screams as it bit him in half.

'I turned in search of Dev, always the most agile of fellows. I watched him dart left and right, up and down, evading two, three, four tentacles at a time. But as he twisted and turned in ever-tighter circles, there was soon nowhere left for him to go. So he stopped, and a dozen tentacles reached for him simultaneously and tore him apart.

'All this time, Kush had swum slowly and steadily through the mayhem, like something dead and adrift. But he had not gone unnoticed. As he was about to break free into clear water, a single tentacle casually wrapped itself around his tailfin, and slowly dragged him back. The squid laughed as Kush suddenly came to life, turning ferociously to sink his tiny teeth into its tentacle, much as an ant might bite an elephant's trunk. And when it could laugh no more, it tightened its grip and Kush was gone too, crushed like an over-ripe tomato in a farmer's fist.

'One by one I watched my best friends die. And I did nothing. It was more than I could bear. I was filled with rage and wanted to avenge them. I felt the current on my back pushing me towards the squid, so I let the water take me. It swept me towards the nearest beast, its mouth already open awaiting its next morsel. One of its tentacles reached out for me, its movement creating a web of currents in the surrounding water that only I could see. With a flick of my fin I let one of them take me, propelling me out of reach. Another tentacle came after me, so I used another current to sweep below the first, then another to rise back over it, leading the chasing tentacle after me. In and out, and up and down I went, each time drawing one tentacle around another. Before long, the tentacles of the squid had become entangled. Other squid arrived to chase me, but I did not tire. Round and round I went, until every squid was entwined with itself and its neighbours. And the more they tried to pull their tentacles free, the tighter the knots binding them together became until, slowly, they squeezed the life out of each other, and became a single, lifeless knot, drifting to the seabed.

'As it came to rest in the sand, I felt no sense of victory, only shame. For I had done nothing to save my friends. I swam with all my might towards the sunlight, desperate to leave the ocean. As I broke the surface I continued upwards, spreading my fins so that the wind might carry me away like a bird. But the sea drew me back, and I began to fall. I closed my eyes as the water exploded in my face. Then I tasted mud, and found myself face down in the thick black puddle at the bottom of our trench. My friends were standing over me, laughing and joking, but wonderfully, *gloriously* . . . alive.

'"Hey, Sanjiv! You were flipping around in that hammock like a fish marooned on the riverbank."

'I leaped up, overjoyed, and threw my arms around them.

'"Get off! You are covering us in mud, you idiot!" But I did not loosen my grip.

'"Clearly, Sanjiv has gone doolally," Kush laughed.

"The thought of being a father has finally tipped him over the edge."

'They could not understand why I was so happy. But to watch your best friends die before your eyes only to see them live again: truly there is no greater feeling. I vowed then, that next time I would not abandon them to their fate.

'That night, I wrote to Old Mr and Mrs Kumar. I promised them, that in the battle that was to come I would not, for one moment, leave their sons' side. I would fight shoulder to shoulder with them. I would protect them and, if necessary, die for them so that they might return home to Bhopal. For in truth, to me, they were more than my best friends. They were my brothers. Such was the certainty in my heart, Amil, that I vowed all this on the eternal honour of our family name.'

22

A Fistful of Dust

Amil had tried to stay awake all night. He did not want the day of the big bet ever to arrive. But it had. The hatch in the workshop had woken him. He climbed down the stairs and sat beside the door, eating his breakfast where it lay. Chunni had drawn another floury smile on the outside of the bowl, the closest she could get to writing him a good luck note. He could barely swallow the food. His stomach felt as though someone had tied a knot in it, so that everything he ate barely made it past his throat. He tried not to think of what might happen to him if he let Jalesh and Hari Laghari down. What if his hand shook with nerves when he released the feather? What if . . . ?

The door jerked open and hit him hard on the knee. Jalesh peered round the door and clicked his fingers sharply. 'Come on, paper-folder, my father has gone off to the tea house. It is time to go.'

As Amil emerged into the sunlight, Jalesh took his arm and marched him to Hari's gambling den for some last-minute rehearsals. Jalesh knocked on several doors along the way, reminding any friends and acquaintances who answered, that the 'Bet of the Century' would be taking place later that day. The rest of the morning was spent in Hari's basement. There, away from curious prying eyes, Amil was made to throw feathers into the old metal bucket which Jalesh intended to use for the main event that afternoon. As always Amil completed each one of the practice tests perfectly. Then, even though he was not at all hungry, Hari insisted that Amil sit and fill his belly before they departed for the square.

'You cannot perform properly if you are weak and trembling with hunger,' he explained, handing him a plate of stale flatbread. 'That would never do.'

As Hari watched over him, Amil forced down every crumb, praying silently to Vayu that the last one would divide in two, and then divide again, and again, so that he could remain there picking at crumbs for ever. But that was not to be, and as his lips closed around the final morsel, Hari lifted him gently to his feet.

The next thing Amil knew, he was in the square, standing alone in the centre of a ring of people, bare to the waist like a miniature boxer awaiting his opponent. Whilst Hari mingled with the crowd discussing odds and assessing the depths of their pockets, Jalesh circled Amil slowly. This was his show, and he was not about to miss the opportunity to taunt a member of the Gujar family in public.

'Before the main event, should you not do some warm-up exercises?' he said. 'Or perhaps we need to prepare you in some way. Shall we get Big Fareed here –' he gestured towards a heavy-set youth currently holding two children half his size in a headlock – 'to grease you with engine oil, perhaps, or attach needles to your fingernails like a fighting bird?'

'Or comb your back!' someone called out, drawing attention to the soft downy hairs on Amil's body. This received the biggest laugh of all.

Amil pressed his lips together and shook his head. Hari nodded to Jalesh from the crowd. He tapped the small bag slung over his shoulder, which contained not only Chunni's life savings but a considerable sum of his own. Everyone they had invited had arrived, he was saying. The 'Bet of the Century' could begin. Jalesh placed the bucket he had brought with him upside down. Then he scooped up a handful of dust and stepped on to it, like an athlete stepping proudly on to the winner's podium. He held his fist aloft and addressed the crowd with the confidence of someone who knew their luck had changed. A hush fell over the square. Jalesh's moment had finally arrived.

'Where the wind blows, nobody knows,' he announced dramatically, opening his fist with a flourish. In an instant, the wind ripped the dust out of his hand and dissolved it, turning it to nothing in the blink of an eye. 'As you can see, the wind around us has a mind of its own,' he declared. 'It is as unpredictable and impossible to control as a rogue elephant. Even so, from twenty paces, Gutless Gujar here will throw a feather . . .' He hesitated. Chunni had arrived, uninvited and unwelcome, and pushed herself to the front of the crowd. As she offered Amil a nod of support, Jalesh forgot all about the bucket. '. . . will throw a feather . . . into the mouth of this volunteer!'

Leaping down from the bucket, he grabbed Chunni by the arms and held her tight in front of him. Immediately, Amil stepped towards her, but Hari yanked him backwards, dragging him twenty paces to the opposite side of the square.

Jalesh and Hari watched and waited, as the crowd buzzed with excitement. Many took a pinch of dust from the ground to conduct their own experiments, with good-natured dust fights breaking out among younger sections of the crowd. Gradually, these ceased as they realised beyond doubt that Jalesh and Hari had no chance of winning their bet, and that there was money here for the taking. Even those few who had heard of Amil's prowess could not believe he could perform such a magical feat. Were these two fools really willing to take bets on the boy? Surely his task was impossible. Hari reached into his shoulder bag and brandished a fistful of money. Even though Amil was now to throw the feather into the mouth of the girl wriggling helplessly in Jalesh's grip, he was unconcerned; he had seen Amil achieve far greater feats. The bet was on.

'We are betting on the boy,' he announced. 'Who will bet against us?'

There was a rush forward. Hari bent down so that he was nose to nose with Amil.

'Remember what happens to soldiers who desert their post. Do not move,' he said, releasing his grip. As Hari flipped open his bag and began taking bets, Amil stared across the square at Chunni, still struggling against her brother's painful grip. In turn, Jalesh's eyes were fixed on the betting frenzy taking place around his new business partner. As he watched, he allowed himself to imagine a future in which they would take Amil to Bombay and Delhi and the other great cities of India. There, far away from his idiot father, he would repeat today's performance not in front of a mere few hundred people, but tens of thousands, perhaps even a million.

Finally, with his pockets as well as his shoulder bag bulging with money, Hari plucked from behind his ear the feather that once belonged to his most prized fighting cockerel, Darwan Singh Negi.

'Jalesh says that you come from a long line of cowards,

so I thought you might like some help from a true hero,' he said, handing the feather to Amil. 'Get ready to throw it.'

Amil stared across at Chunni, pinned helplessly by her arms by her beast of a brother. 'Jalesh,' he called out, 'why can I not aim for some other target. Why Chunni?'

Jalesh stared down at his sister, then back at Amil. 'Why not? She killed our mother, it is the least she can do.'

'That is a filthy lie,' cried Chunni, defiantly. 'I did not kill her. She died!'

'It is the truth,' Jalesh spat back at her. 'Pappa told me. Many times. That is why I hate you so much. That is why we *both* hate you.'

At these words Chunni's steady, determined face dissolved. Like a mud mask exposed to the blazing sun, it began to crack and flake and then fall away, to reveal a terrified, miserable little girl underneath. Her head tipped back and her mouth dropped open as though she were about to catch the monsoon rains on her tongue.

'My father does *not* hate me!' she screamed, tears rolling down her face. She tried to twist herself free – 'Let me go, *let me go!*' – but Jalesh merely dug his fingernails deeper into her arm. With his other hand, he pinched her cheeks together hard, forcing her mouth wide open.

'Time to perform your little party trick, paper-folder!' he called across to Amil. 'Throw the feather now, unless you would prefer a beating.'

Chunni's tears were too much for Amil to bear, and his own eyes filled up. But not with tears; with anger. If it was not bad enough that every rupee she had ever scrimped and saved had been stolen, he was now expected to humiliate her in front of every ruffian in Bhopal. Without thinking he grabbed a fistful of dust, and sent it spiralling across the square in a perfect triple loop to explode in Jalesh's face. Then, before Hari could stop him, he charged at Jalesh. As he reached him, the toe of one of his oversized sandals caught the ground, pitching him forward so that he headbutted Jalesh in the stomach with all the force of a large, angry goat. The crowd winced. As her brother flew backwards, blinded and winded, Chunni twisted free of his grip. She grabbed Amil's hand and they ran. Hari made a desperate diving lunge for them as they disappeared through the crowd, catching nothing more than a mouthful of dirt as he crashed to the ground. At the same moment, Amil finally released the prize feather into the wind, hearing the raucous delight of the crowd behind him as it rose beyond the reach of Hari's outstretched fingertips and drifted down into their midst, far away from its original target.

At first, no one followed them. Instead, the crowd applauded the extraordinary, almost superhuman skill, which Amil had demonstrated at Jalesh's expense, before surging towards Jalesh and Hari to collect their winnings. As Amil and Chunni ran out of the square, the air behind them erupted with the sound of shouts and screams, as fists flew and arguments raged over whether the bet was lost or whether, indeed, it had even taken place. Amil could think of nowhere else to go but the attic, so he and Chunni ran as fast as they could back to the workshop. They arrived just as Mr Kumar was stepping into his house, having returned from the tea house in search of an early dinner. He turned as they flashed past him, but by the time he reached the workshop door they had disappeared into the attic, and closed the hatch behind them.

23
Under Siege

'What is going on, Chunni? Come out of there, now! You should be in the house, cooking my dinner.'

Mr Kumar climbed the rotten steps as far as he dared, and reached up to push at the attic door. But despite his increasingly vigorous efforts, it barely moved. On the other side, Amil and Chunni had already dragged the heavy trunk over the hatch and sat huddled together on top of it, their arms intertwined to steady each other as the attic door trembled beneath them. Then there was more shouting from below as Jalesh ran into the workshop. He was bruised and bloodied, and whilst his pockets may now have been empty, his heart was full-to-bursting with rage.

Amil and Chunni could hear him explaining his version of events to his father. How Amil had stolen the money he had been saving to buy back Kumar and Sons' old printing press. How he and Chunni had gone to the square to gamble it all away.

'The Gujar boy has betrayed us, just like his great-grandfather,' he told him. 'He has lost all our money.'

The story fitted perfectly with everything Mr Kumar wished to believe about Amil. Were they to be for ever cursed by these low-caste Gujars?

'Then get up there and sort the boy out,' he growled.

Jalesh did not need to be told twice. He leaped up the steps and began slamming his already bloodied fists into the attic door like sledgehammers, turning it red.

'I am going to kill you, Gujar, do you hear? I am going to kill you!'

When Jalesh tired, Mr Kumar threw himself back at the task, pounding the door with his palms.

'Come out, you thief! Come out or I will rip this door off its hinges.'

Above, as each frenzied onslaught increased in intensity the trunk jumped around beneath Amil and Chunni, threatening to dislodge them from their perch. But they hung on to each other and kept their balance. The hatch held firm. Mr Kumar panted cool air on to his swollen hands. Clearly, Amil and Chunni would have to be coaxed down. But that would be impossible whilst his son was there baying for their blood. So, he sent Jalesh away to bathe his wounds.

For a few moments the workshop fell silent. Then, Mr Kumar dragged a plastic chair slowly across the stone floor to the foot of the steps. He sat sprawled in it for several minutes, dabbing an endless stream of sweat from his face as his chest rose and fell. Finally, when he had recovered his breath, he addressed the attic door.

'Your brother has gone, Chunni. It is safe to come down now,' he told her.

Chunni did not believe him. 'You will beat me,' she said.

'I will beat the boy, but not you. Not if you open the hatch now.'

On top of the trunk, Chunni shook her head at Amil. She did not want him to take a beating for her.

When no reply came, Mr Kumar appealed to Amil directly.

'This is all your fault, Gujar. You have poisoned my daughter against me. If she does not come down now to cook my dinner, I shall hold you responsible. Such a beating awaits you, boy. If you have so much as a shred of courage, you will at least spare Chunni the same fate.'

Chunni gripped Amil's hand. 'Do not listen to him.'

There was a pause as Mr Kumar heaved himself back on to the steps. He pushed hard against the hatch, but nothing had changed, so he pounded it several times with his clenched fist. He decided to appeal to Amil's sense of honour.

'You cannot spend the night up there with my daughter,' he told him. 'It is forbidden. If you do not come down now you will bring eternal shame on Chunni and her family.

Is that what you want?' Amil knew how it felt to be shamed, and he did not want it for Chunni. He stood up, but she pulled him back on to the trunk and held him tight.

'You cannot go down there, Amil,' she whispered.

But Mr Kumar had not given up. Whilst clearly the boy had no intention of behaving honourably – he was a Gujar, after all – perhaps he could appeal to his daughter's sense of duty. Or maybe a simple bribe might persuade her.

'But who will cook my dinner, Chunni? That is woman's work. Do you want your father to starve to death? If you come down now and make a tasty chicken curry for me, I will forgive you. I will even give you five rupees to buy ribbons for your hair.'

But nothing could weaken Chunni's resolve to stay at Amil's side, and when his various ploys to coax them down failed, Mr Kumar made one last frantic effort to break in, attacking the hatch like a wild beast. The pounding of his fists shook the trunk for several minutes. When the hatch failed to give way, Mr Kumar used the plastic chair as a battering ram, repeatedly hammering it into the wood before hurling it, with a loud clatter, against the workshop floor in frustration. For a few moments after that, Amil and Chunni heard nothing but the pounding of their own hearts. Then Mr Kumar climbed the last few steps to press his lips against the hatch and hiss his final threat. 'Come out now, Gujar, or I will return in the morning to rip this door off its hinges and beat you both to within inches of your lives.' Two feet away, perched on the trunk, Chunni clamped an arm around Amil's waist and a hand over his mouth. The matter was not for debate. She would not let him go down those steps, even to save herself.

Finally, they heard a jangling of keys as Mr Kumar locked the attic door and prepared to retreat. As he descended the steps, one of them snapped under his weight, sending him sprawling to the floor. As he lay on his back like an upturned tortoise, he screamed up at the hatch.

'See what you made me do, boy. I nearly broke my neck on these rotten steps. Damn you, Gujar! Damn your whole cursed family!'

Then the workshop door slammed shut, and Amil and Chunni were alone. They sat in silence as the light faded and the attic fell into semi-darkness. Amil retrieved his torch from where it lay in the hammock, along with Sanjiv's journal. By the time he turned it on, Chunni had fallen asleep and lay curled up on top of the trunk. He too was exhausted, his eyes and his heart heavy. He felt as though he had been in a battle, and that only the attic door had saved him from death at the hands of an enemy who truly hated him. He knew that a proper soldier would use the time between battles to tend to his weapons, fill his stomach and, if possible, catch some sleep before the following day's onslaught. But Amil did not want to sleep. He knew that when Mr Kumar and Jalesh returned in the morning, they would come better armed, and the hatch would not hold. He shone his torch at the skylight, the only possible means of escape. But he knew he could not abandon Chunni, or take her away from her family, and he had given Uncle Ravi his word that he would not run away again. Besides, where could he go – he had no idea how to find his mother and father, and even his uncle had gone. With a sense of impending doom gnawing like rats at his empty stomach, he vowed to stay awake and make the most of what he feared might be his last night alive.

He took up Sanjiv's journal and climbed into the hammock. Where was his great-grandfather? Surely all the battering on the attic door would have woken him. He shone the torch at the pile of rags in the corner but saw no movement. It was not until he turned his torch to the pages of Sanjiv's story that he heard the rags stir.

A sleepy and dishevelled head emerged into the moonlight.

'I heard shouting,' the old man yawned, 'It reminded me of the trenches.'

Amil said nothing, for in truth he had no desire to speak to his great-grandfather.

'But it is fortunate that you woke me,' Sanjiv continued, sniffing the air. 'We are about to reach the most important part of the story.'

Before he could continue, Amil's shoulders began to heave up and down.

'What did you *do*, Pardadaji? Why am I here?' he sobbed. 'It is not fair!'

For a few seconds, Sanjiv bowed his head, as though the pain and regret inside it were too heavy for him to carry any longer. Then, slowly, he looked up at Amil.

'You must turn the page,' he said.

24

The Lunatic Soldier

'On the morning of the attack I stayed close to Kush and his brothers, determined to fight shoulder to shoulder with them as I had vowed to do. Having stood in the mud for days on end, we knew that our attack would begin soon. But first our enemy would endure the wrath of our artillery. As a screaming hell of fire and metal was unleashed to break down their defences, all but our lookouts squatted with our backs against the trench walls and our hands over our ears. The barrage continued without pause, each shell crashing into the enemy trenches and the barbed wire protecting them from unwanted visitors. The shells had long ago ceased disfiguring the landscape, for there was nothing of it left to disfigure. Instead, the shells were simply moving mountains of mud and flesh around from one place to another. The enemy would be underground in their dug-out shelters, but the shells would arrive on top of them by the thousand, making craters, within craters, within craters, all the time digging down like a wild boar searching for grubs. Those that survived would face our gas. After that, they would face us.

'An hour later the bombardment stopped. Backs were straightened, and periscopes raised to inspect the condition of the enemy defences. Within a few moments, the order came from the major general to open the valves on the gas cylinders. The taps were duly turned, and gas began to hiss out in long streams towards the enemy trenches, all the time spreading wider until, half way across No Man's Land they converged to become a single pale-green sea, flowing as one towards our foe. I pitied the poor souls on the other side. The gas would roll into their trenches. There it would remain, as the rest rolled onwards, with us behind it in clear air, ready to complete its work. Those who survived the gas would stumble from their trenches to escape, blinded by their masks, there to meet the ends of our bayonets. The life of Captain Bradbury and our fallen comrades would be avenged on this day. The wind was true and steady, reports said, masks would merely impede our ability to crush a weakened enemy. We would not repeat their mistake.

'And so we waited for the gas to reach them, and do our work for us. Then the order came to line up beside the ladders that would take us up and over to meet the enemy. Kush was first in line, bayonet in hand, ready to fix, followed by Deepak and Dev, shifting restlessly from foot to foot. I was behind them, leaning out to watch the new captain on the other side of the ladder. With the whistle around his neck, ready and waiting on the end of its cord, he stared nervously down at his watch. Then he raised his hand and, on his command, a dozen men along the line crawled out of the trench to turn off the valves. The moment they slithered back, he gave the order we had all been waiting for: "Fix bayonets!"

'As the last of the gas made its way towards the enemy, the hairs on the back of my neck began to prickle. I was overcome with a sense of foreboding, worse even than the prospect of battle. Something was wrong with the wind. Without thinking, I pushed my way to the ladder, and before Kush and the captain could stop me I had scrambled out of the trench.

The captain's orderly called up to me. "Gujar, Gujar! Return to your post!"

'Then, I recognised the voices of Kush and his brothers. "Sanjiv, you will be shot. This is suicide. Get down!"

'But the gas cloud between me and the enemy protected me from their snipers. As they continued to call after me I threw my kit and ammunition to the ground, and began tearing at the buttons of my uniform, stripping down to the waist. I needed to know what the wind had in store for us. I stretched out my arms and opened my fingers. As I felt its cool breath on my arms and back, I lifted my head to observe the drift and curl of the clouds, and feel the wind tickle the hairs inside my nose and ears, bringing with it scents of places from which it had come, and subtle notes and harmonies which whispered of its intentions. And those intentions were very clear to me. As I opened my eyes I knew, with a certainty that plunged my heart into black fathomless despair, what was about to happen, and what I must do. I turned my back on the cloud of gas and ran to appeal to the captain.

'"Sir, the gas will not reach the enemy. It will turn and kill us all. We must put on our masks, otherwise it is us who will perish, not them."

'But the captain ignored my words and sent Kush up the ladder after me. "Get that madman down!" he barked. "Gujar! Pick up your weapon and fall back in line. That is an order."

'But I did not return to the trench. I knew that only seconds remained before the captain and all my friends and comrades would die, killed by the poisonous tentacles of the monster we had unleashed, or by the hideous masked hordes that inevitably would follow through to finish its grim task. As Kush took hold of me I turned to him. Surely, he would understand.

'"The wind is about to change," I told him. "We must put on our masks."

'But he shook his head. "That is preposterous. Surely

237

you cannot imagine that the wind is on the side of the Germans. You must steady yourself, Sanjiv. It is not our place to question orders. We must do our duty and obey them." He gripped my shoulders. "Remember, it is only our sense of honour which separates us from the cockroaches. I will stand by you as I have always done. We are the Bo-Peeps; we will be victorious, you will see."

'But I knew that the wind took no sides. For a moment, I thought it would indeed be better to die with my friends than disobey an order. But the gods had given me a gift that could save the lives of my comrades, and I had sworn to their mother and father that I would protect them. So I twisted free. Kush gave chase, calling me back. But unencumbered by my heavy kit I was able to outrun him. I ran semi-naked along the side of the trench, pleading with the lines of soldiers waiting to climb the ladders. "Put on your masks! The gas will turn."

'Some made a grab for my ankles, calling me a coward, a deserter, even a traitor, as they tried to pull me back into the trench. Others laughed at the semi-naked lunatic, released to brighten the last remaining moments of their lives. But most ignored me, their minds transfixed on the horrors that lay ahead of them. Still I did not give up. I retraced my steps, arriving back at my starting point just as the captain raised his whistle to his lips. I felt the wind turn. "Put on your masks!" I screamed. But it was too late.

The whistle had blown, and suddenly my voice was drowned out by the shouts of men going to war. "Kush! Deepak! Dev! All of you! Listen to me."

'But they did not hear me. Up the ladders they came, streaming from the trench in long dark lines, like columns of ants marching out of their nest. As they spread out, I tried to stop them, running along from man to man to push him back, pleading, screaming what I knew, clawing at their tunics until my fingers were broken and bloodied.

'"Your duty is to live. Not to hand your life to the enemy," I told them. But nothing could dissuade them from their course. Every man brushed past me as though I did not exist. Their minds were impenetrable, their eyes fixed ahead as firmly as their bayonets, resigned to whatever fate lay in store for them. Little time remained for me to save them. The cloud had turned and was rolling towards us like a sickly green tidal wave. The bullet of a lucky sniper cut through the cloud to kill a soldier next to me. He fell dead at my feet. I reached into his backpack and put on his mask. Then, as my friends marched heroically into the gas cloud to carry out their orders, I plunged in after them.

'But there was no heroic outcome. One by one, after a few paces, men fell to their knees, their eyes rolling back into their heads, their lungs consumed with the froth and poison that was drowning them. A few whose knees refused to buckle lurched on towards the enemy wire, and the waiting machine guns. Still more ran screaming, blind, their faces blistered, out of the cloud towards our line. Unable to escape the gas already inside them, they too, fell. And yet, even this did not deter the stragglers, who continued onward into the cloud, unable to disobey their orders and turn back. Then they too were gone, and the cloud was full of muffled cries and screams, as the Germans, masked and full of menace, followed the cloud towards our lines to take home their advantage.

I searched for my friends amid the mayhem, squinting through the portholes in my mask, as the gas attacked my body like a million burning prickles, turning it to blisters. Bodies lay in their wispy green shrouds all around me, but none of them I knew. And then I found Kush, on his hands and knees, frothing at the mouth and choking as he clawed at the lifeless bodies of his brothers. I grabbed his kit belt and began to drag him backwards through the mud, weaving a ragged, muddy furrow around the bodies of men still clutching their throats, lying as cold and grey and lifeless as the pebbles on Brighton beach. And then Kush, my best friend Kush, tipped his head back and looked at me. Except that his eyes had no life in them. They were rolled up in his head. His mouth was open but he had ceased breathing through it. I laid him down in the mud, just as row upon row of black-snouted assailants emerged from the mist, bayonets fixed, and advanced towards our deserted trench. I wanted to die there, with my friends, to charge alone at the Germans barechested and barehanded to avenge them. Then, too late, the order to retreat sounded. I no longer had any reason to disobey, so I retraced my steps to retrieve my rifle and my kitbag, and stumbled back over the trench to the safety of our lines beyond. By the time I fell into the arms of a stretcher-bearer, I could no longer feel the wind, or even hear it. My head was full of screams.'

Amil's great-grandfather lay back in the pile of rags, staring up at the ceiling.

'That is what happened, Amil. It is true that I did not march forward with the Kumars into battle. And it is true that I was not by their side when they fell. My semi-naked lunacy was witnessed by the major general and his officers perched high on an observation ridge behind our lines. Through their binoculars they saw nothing but a man losing his mind to fear and refusing to fight. A shameful coward, whose family ever since has been paying for his sins. That is why you are here, Amil.'

'But why did you not show them?' Amil said. 'Why did you not take off your shirt and demonstrate your gift to prove that you tried to save them?'

'I could not,' Sanjiv replied. 'The gas took away more than my friends that day. It took away my gift, too.'

Very slowly, he peeled off his shirt, and rolled on to his face. Amil shone the torch on to his great-grandfather's back and recoiled instantly, as his beam landed on a livid sea of boiling red blisters.

'You see,' said Sanjiv, 'I could no longer feel the wind against my skin, because the gas had burned it all away.'

For a moment, Amil was silent. He shone the torch over to Chunni, still sleeping soundly on top of the trunk.

'But your journal, surely someone must have read it.'

Carefully, his great-grandfather turned himself over to face Amil. As he shook his head, tears began to roll silently down his cheeks.

'Not even my son,' he sighed. 'Even though my belongings were returned to Bhopal, they were so deeply ingrained with shame that they remained untouched, leaving the truth unread. Until now. You are the first person to know what really happened that day.'

Amil turned the page. As he did so, a long-forgotten bookmark dropped on to his chest: a cigarette card. He read the inscription of heroic deeds on the back, then turned it over to look at the portrait of the Indian soldier who had carried them out. Darwan Singh Negi V.C.

He turned the card around in his fingers thoughtfully for a few seconds.

'This is the card that Mr Kumar has been looking for,' he said.

Sanjiv gasped.

'Then perhaps you are not the first person to have discovered my journal, after all,' he replied.

'But Pardadaji, that means he must know the truth. That you are not a coward. That I should not be here.'

'That man would not recognise the truth if it reared up like a cobra and bit him on the backside,' said Sanjiv. 'Can you imagine such a bitter, slothful man admitting to his family and everyone he knows, that his endless failures have been of his own making, not mine? For him, the shame of falling below the high standards expected of his caste would be too much to bear. Far better to consider my journal to be nothing but preposterous lies, concocted by a lowly coward trying to avoid the ultimate punishment for his crimes. Or, better still, lock it away and forget about it altogether.'

Amil nodded. His great-grandfather was right, Mr Kumar could never admit the truth. Not to himself. Not to anyone. He returned his tired eyes to the journal. The hand-tied cotton stitching now visible down the crease told him that he had reached its centre. Yet the blank pages beyond told him that this was not the middle of Sanjiv's story, but the end.

'Read it all, Amil. Like my son was meant to.'

So, as Mr Kumar had done secretly many years before him, Amil read the last written words of Sanjiv Gujar.

When he had finished, he closed the book, and looked towards the corner of the room. His great-grandfather was almost gone. As he sank slowly beneath his sea of rags, the cries and screams of battle rose to fill Amil's head, and chased him deep into his sleep.

25
Escape

'Wake up, Amil. *Wake up!*'

Chunni was shaking the side of Amil's hammock. He opened his eyes and looked at her, then at the journal resting on his chest, then at the pile of rags in the corner. There was no sign of Sanjiv, but the screams he had described were still there, and they were coming from the street below. Then another sound joined them – the siren from the pesticide plant, screaming its warning to the citizens of Bhopal. Amil sniffed the midnight air – something was different, amiss. At that moment, everything his great-grandfather had taught him, and everything his uncle had told him, became one thought. He knew what he must do. He leaped down from the hammock.

'We must run like the wind,' he told Chunni. 'Chachaji warned me. If the siren sounds, we must run, or we will die.' Amil dragged the trunk from over the hatch and tried to lift the attic door. 'We are still locked in,' he said. As he searched around frantically for something he could use to break open the hatch, Chunni pushed the trunk against the wall to look out of the skylight.

'People are everywhere,' she cried, 'screaming and running for their lives. And there is a horrible yellow cloud creeping over the slums towards us.' Amil spun around, searching the room for some means of escape. And then his eyes fell on the hammock. In a few seconds, Chunni had helped him unhook it. Together, they secured one end to the old window catch and lowered the rest out of the skylight.

'You go first,' said Amil. Chunni hesitated. 'It is strong enough to carry a horse,' he told her. 'We have to hurry.'

Chunni climbed on to the trunk. She hoisted her dress up to her knees and reversed out of the skylight, digging her fingernails into the rough canvas as she inched her way down the sloping roof. Then she was over the edge, climbing straight down against the back wall of the workshop. Although the hammock barely reached halfway to the ground, she managed to hang from the bottom strap, steadying herself for a few seconds before letting herself drop into the lamp-lit street below. Then it was Amil's turn. He leaped on to the trunk.

'Take my kitbag, Amil, it is all yours now.' The voice had come from behind him. Amil spun round.

'Pardadaji! *Pardadaji!*' He ran to the corner of the room

and dug deep into the pile of rags like a dog scrabbling for a bone. Rats, disturbed from their nest, scattered everywhere. But Sanjiv was not there. He returned to the trunk, threw the journal into Sanjiv's kitbag and slung it over his shoulder. With one last look back, he climbed out of the skylight.

Chunni was waiting for him as he dropped to the ground. They ran as fast as they could to the front of the workshop, arriving as Mr Kumar and Jalesh staggered out of the house, coughing and retching. As they stumbled into the street Amil saw the yellow cloud inside, rolling slowly towards the front door from the back of the house, where it had crept in through an open window. A light breeze flowing down the street was keeping it at bay, but in a few seconds he knew the cloud would cross the street to meet them. Mr Kumar and Jalesh were both bent double, their hands clasped to their knees as they fought for breath. Jalesh looked up to see Amil standing beside Chunni. He straightened up to lunge at him, swinging a fist wildly in Amil's direction, hitting nothing but the air which was about to give way to the oncoming cloud. Then his knees buckled and he fell to the ground, choking.

Instinctively, Amil bent down to help him. 'Jalesh, you must come with me. I can help us all escape.'

But Mr Kumar sent him sprawling to the ground.

'Leave him alone. Have you not done enough?' he

croaked. He bent down to pick up his son just as a tide of people swept past them, screaming and wailing as they fled from the direction of the pesticide plant.

'It is coming this way. Run for your lives!'

With Jalesh cradled like a limp rag doll in his arms, Mr Kumar turned his back on his daughter and stepped into the human flow.

Amil leaped to his feet and grabbed Chunni's hand. 'They are running the wrong way, do not follow them.'

But she was too strong for him. She twisted free and plunged into the crowd after her father, reaching out to grasp his shirt to pull him back. 'Father, Amil knows which way to go. We must trust him.'

But Mr Kumar did not stop. He did not even turn to acknowledge the one person who truly cared for him, who had always looked after him and who was, even now, trying to save his life. She continued tugging at his shirt, pleading with him to turn around, but he could neither hear nor see her. She did not exist. Instead, with his glazed eyes fixed straight ahead, he brushed her away like a fly, and pushed forward. And then he was beyond her reach, and then gone, she knew, for ever.

A hand gripped her wrist. 'We have to get to the other side of the street; I need to climb the lamppost,' Amil told her.

As the panicking crowd continued to push them

forward, they elbowed their way through it like swimmers crossing a fast-flowing river that was trying to sweep them away. Their way was blocked by people pushing bicycles, cattle that had lost their owners, people who had stumbled choking to the ground, or who kneeled in the dust, mourning stricken loved ones. To his surprise, Amil could feel the ebb and flow of the crowd, much as he could feel the wind. He knew that if he and Chunni did not reach the other side of the street at least a pace ahead of the lamppost, the crowd would sweep them past it. And they would never get back. He tightened his grip on Chunni and sharpened his elbows.

'Come on, Chunni!' He pulled her behind him, lunging for the lamppost the moment it came within reach. He wrapped his arm around it and pulled Chunni close. 'Give me a hand up,' Amil said. Chunni nodded weakly, then cupped her hands in front of her knees. Amil stepped up to grasp the lamppost and hoist himself up. Then he wrapped his legs around the post and began to climb. 'Wait there; do not let go,' he told her.

He reached the top in a few seconds. Raising himself above the glare of the streetlights, he could at last see the sky. He could also see the bright orange windsock flying above the pesticide plant, protruding like a giant periscope from the sea of sickly yellow gas hugging the surrounding ground. The wind was blowing it north. But Amil knew that the windsock merely showed the present. It could not predict the future. And he needed to know where the wind was about to go.

He twisted and turned at the top of the lamppost, observing, for as long as he dared, the innocent drift of the clouds above him, and every deadly wisp and curl of the gas cloud below, as it rolled through the nooks and crannies of his city. Then his eyes turned to examine the buildings, the lampposts, the width and pitch of the streets and alleyways through which people were running. The wind pursued them, like an innocent courier delivering death to every living thing it touched, its grim task diverted only momentarily by the obstacles that lay in its path. Already, as he had known it would, a few streets ahead Amil could see the gas drifting around to encircle the fleeing crowds and cut off their escape. Chunni's father and brother were among them, running straight into its fatal embrace. Even though he had tried and failed to save them, just as his great-grandfather had tried and failed to save Kush and his brothers, the purpose of his gift was clear to him now. It was to save the life of Chunni Kumar. There had to be a way out.

He tore off his shirt and stuffed it into the kitbag as he took one last look around. Then, with the picture of the city in his head he tightened his legs around the pole, stretched out his arms, and closed his eyes. Leaning back, he began to feel the wind weaving in and out of his fingers, and caress the army of fine hairs over his back as it whispered its intentions to his skin. As it did so, the picture came to life. A vision of the future unfolded behind his eyes, showing him and Chunni zigzagging through the streets, their escape route drawn like a pencil line through a printed maze, towards an exit on the other side – a gateway to the clean, safe air beyond. The gateway would open only for a few seconds. They would have to run like the wind.

Amil scrambled down the lamppost. By the time he jumped down beside Chunni, the gas cloud had spread outwards from the Kumars' house and crept up the street. It had almost reached them, yet he knew they could not run directly away from it, like Chunni's father. They needed to cross its path, fight their way back across the river of people so that they could run at right angles to it. That was the only way out. As they waded back into the crowd Amil screamed and shouted, trying to divert as many people as he could from their path. But no one would listen to him. No one followed. Instead, they stared ahead half-blinded, their burning, tear-filled eyes fixed in panic on the back of the person in front of them.

As they approached a crossroads the street narrowed like the neck of a bottle, forcing the crowd to a halt. Amil pulled Chunni free and led her down a side alley, as behind them, more and more desperate men, women and children crushed up against each other on the main street, unable to move forward. Finally, the river of people burst its banks and spilled down the alleyway after Amil and Chunni. Amil ran with such unhesitating confidence that those behind him followed instinctively. Led by Amil, with Chunni tightly in his grip, the crowd zigzagged through Bhopal's maze of streets and alleyways like a meandering stream, unaware of the direction in which they were heading. All they could do was follow the person leading them. And that person was Amil.

When they reached another crossroads, Amil stopped. He spun around, looking up at the sky. It was almost time. From the muffled screams behind him, he could tell that the cloud had followed and was beginning to overtake them. Ahead and to the right, the cloud was creeping slowly towards them. As he hesitated, the crowd fled on, turning left towards the only clear air they could see. But Amil knew that the gas would be there to ambush them. They were running to their deaths. He jumped on to a low wall and screamed at them to turn back. But no one heard him. No one listened.

Suddenly, a boy about Jalesh's age recognised Amil from the square. He began dragging his parents towards him, refusing to follow them.

'That is the boy from the square,' he told them, pointing.

'He knows which way the wind blows.' His parents ignored him, and tried to force him to go with them. But he was too big to be told, wrenching his arm free, screaming for his life. 'We have to follow him!'

'Your son is right.' Another man, his daughter draped over his arms, had recognised Amil too. He told his neighbour. As Amil led Chunni over the crossroads and directly towards the cloud, others joined them.

'The boy knows which way to go. The boy knows which way to go.' The words spread like a promise through the crowd, and in seconds the trickle of people following Amil became a stream. A hundred yards from the cloud he stopped. Waiting. Behind him the screams grew louder as people converged on the crossroads, the encircling gas having forced them back from the adjoining streets. Soon the stream of people behind Amil would become a torrent. But still it was not time. Ahead of them, with nothing visible through it but the sulphurous glow of a flickering streetlamp, lay a wall of gas, thick and impenetrable. It hung there, defiant, daring any to venture towards it. Behind Amil, people stared, waiting, praying that they might wake up from the nightmare in which they found themselves. Others fell to their knees, coughing and retching, their lungs on fire. And then the cloud began to roll towards them, spewing yet more blinded and stumbling bodies into the street from the shops and houses in its path. As it advanced, some people behind Amil ran back into the cloud that had been chasing them, desperate to reach help for the children dying in their arms, or find water for their burning lungs, or climb aboard a bus or lorry that would transport them to safety. Many more stayed where they were, too dazed or burdened with loved ones to run, unable to escape not only the gas, but the muffled cries of those it was torturing to death a mere street away. As the gas rolled menacingly towards them from both directions, they pressed ever tighter behind Amil.

But he stood firm. He squeezed Chunni's hand. 'We have to run straight towards the cloud.' He looked up. 'The wind is about to change, I know it,' he told her.

The moon appeared between two clouds, casting a dim yellow light. It was enough for Amil to see the twists and curls of the outer fringes of the gas cloud and the milky silhouettes of the buildings lining the street. The cloud in front of them began to move towards them faster now.

Amil reached into the kitbag and pulled out Sanjiv's old gas mask. 'You must put this on.' Before she could protest he had reached up and thrust it over Chunni's head. Quickly, he tucked it in around her neck. 'Get ready,' he said.

The screams around them intensified as, one by one,

the streetlamps in both directions were reduced to no more than pinpricks of light as the gas clouds converged on each other. Blotting out light. Blotting out lives. Amil turned to those behind him. 'Follow me,' he cried, 'we must run now.' He tightened his grip on Chunni, and with breath held tight and eyes like slits, charged towards the cloud in front of him as though he meant to run straight through it. The boy and his parents were right behind him, followed by others who had heard of Amil's mastery of the wind. Then, as the wind behind them quickened, sending the gas cloud after them like a deadly breaking wave, the flood of people following Amil and Chunni became a stampede. The boy's reputed mastery of the wind had become their only hope, the lone piece of driftwood that would stop them from drowning.

Behind Amil, the sound of screams and pounding feet seemed to merge into a single roar, like a tsunami of fear and panic about to break over him. There was no turning back now. He ran on to meet the cloud head on, uncertain of its depth, certain only that the wind behind them was about to blow a hole in it wide enough for them to run through.

'Hold your breath, Chunni!'

Amil timed his run perfectly. The moment he and the gas cloud met, the street widened, speeding the wind at his back. As the last lungfuls of clean air overtook them, it lifted over the cloud. And as it rose, it sucked the gas cloud upwards from the centre, so that it parted like a pair of curtains before being hauled into the sky.

Higher up, as Amil knew it would, another current flowing down from the hills would halt the flow and the gas cloud would begin to sink back to hug the ground, and its victims. But through the temporary gateway clean air beckoned, higher ground to escape the pursuing monster. As the cloud parted it revealed its deadly harvest: Mr Sharma lying in front of his shop, cradling his wife, men and women and children and babies, and cattle and dogs and cats and rats, and birds fallen from the sky – all strewn across the street among a thousand discarded shoes. Amil and those behind him stumbled over and around them much as water tumbles over rocks, twisting and turning to find a way through.

And then Amil's oversized sandals betrayed him, and he tripped. As he fell to join the lifeless bodies in the dust, Chunni was ripped from his grasp and carried away in the human current, as a thousand stampeding feet pressed Amil into the open graveyard in which he lay. Each time he tried to raise himself up, a foot would press him back into the dirt, face to face with the dead.

At last the battering ceased and Amil forced himself up on to his knees. Around him all was still. He was the only living thing. Ahead and behind him, the gas had returned in silence. The curtains had almost closed, and the gas was about to come for him again. He tried to stand but the monster had rubbed chillies into his eyes so that he could barely see. He stumbled and fell back among the bodies. Too weak to lift himself up, he reached out to unwrap a length of sari from his glassy-eyed neighbour and stretch it over his mouth. But wisps of gas reached through the fibres and began to push down into his lungs like burning hot tentacles. He remembered how Sanjiv had described lying on the battlefield among the dead, with a demon's foul breath blowing in his face. He could feel it too. Perhaps if he closed his eyes, like his great-grandfather, he too would wake up in a palace. A palace, no less! At least, he told himself, if he closed them, they might not burn quite so fiercely. So, slowly, he let his eyelids fall. As they closed, the last thing he saw was the face of a ghost, staring down at him through huge porthole eyes. Then the face spoke to him, and he heard Chunni's voice.

26

The Last Bo-Peep

2 014: Brighton beach. A man stands barefoot on the pebbles, trousers rolled tight to the calf as the surf hisses around his ankles. His eyes are yellow, rolled up into his skull as if to escape some unseen horror. He cannot see the kite he is flying. He does not need to. The wind lapping the fine hairs on his back tells him all he needs to know. He twists the line between his fingers. Above him, his kite wheels round, then spirals upward. A dozen seagulls follow this strange blue bird. With its long winding tail spiralling behind it, it seems to know the wind as well as they do. Better. Whereas they merely respond to its ebbs and flows, the kite predicts them, leading the way, always one breath ahead. Two more kites join the first. A dogfight ensues, as two miniature apprentices test their raw gift against the mastery of their father. But they cannot catch him. He and the wind are one, and the wind cannot be caught.

As the kites continue their merry dance, further up the beach, cradled in a bank of warm pebbles, a third child, the oldest, sits beside his mother. Today is his tenth birthday, and his mother has just told him a story. But it is not quite finished. From her embroidered canvas bag, she takes out the journal that, until today, belonged to the boy's father. She hands it to her son. He thanks her, and she smiles. Now, the journal written by his great-great-grandfather Sanjiv Gujar belongs to him.

As he opens it the wind puffs up, turning over the yellowed pages like invisible fingers until it reaches the centre of the book. Here, at a place marked by an old cigarette card, the boy reads the final, faded testimony of an honourable man. Written on the eve of his execution, it is the truth to those who would not listen, and to those who might one day, like him, understand.

To my son

If I had watched them set their bayonets
true and square to certain death,
and let them stride unknowing to their fate,

If I had watched the gas return
to sear their lungs with every breath,
and stilled my voice until it was too late,

If I had watched in silence as they fell
to gasp their final gurgling breath,
and never tried to drag them back from hell,

Then gladly, I would die a coward's death.

But I did not go quietly that day.
I raged and roared till I was hoarse:
'The wind will turn! Put on your masks or fall!'

With bloodied nails and dug-in heels
I fought to drag them from their course,
but every one refused to hear my call,

And onward marched to meet the turning tide,
to drown beneath that pale-green sea,
as, cradled in my arms, mouths choking wide,
they fought their final enemy.

Until, with frozen face and lifeless swivelled eyes,
each man I laid to sleep.
And the earth no longer echoed to their cries,
but only to my own, the last Bo-Peep.

Sanjiv Gujar, 1915

Afterword

In 1984, as a young graphic designer, I was freelancing in a design consultancy in London. One day, I was given a black-and-white photograph of an Indian farmer standing in a ploughed field, and asked to arrange it alongside some text for the back of a pesticide leaflet. The client was Union Carbide – who until then I had only ever associated with car batteries – and the leaflet was for a pesticide similar to the one manufactured in the company's plant in Bhopal, India.

Halfway through completing my layout task, the Bhopal disaster was announced on the radio and I was instructed to stop work. Although my connection to India, to Union Carbide and the disaster itself is therefore extremely minor, that day stuck with me and has inspired me to write about it decades later. It was the first time I realised that in many parts of the world western companies still put profits before the health and safety of local people. Thus, my book is intended to bring this issue, as exemplified tragically by the Bhopal disaster, to the attention of a new generation of children in the best way I know how.

In writing this book, I have benefited greatly from the scholarly work of others, who in their painstaking accounts of the 1984 Bhopal disaster and the experiences of Indian soldiers during the First World War, have helped provide a factual backdrop against which to set the fictional events of this story. In this respect, I would like to recommend *Five Past Midnight in Bhopal* by Dominique Lapierre & Javier Moro, and *Sepoys in the Trenches* by Gordon Corrigan.

Where I have veered from the factual accuracy of these and other sources, I have done so for the purposes of the story. For example, I have simplified the complex safety issues leading to the disaster at the Bhopal plant, and changed the real 9th Bhopal Infantry to a fictitious 'Bhopal Infantry' to avoid any specific historical comparisons. Additionally, contrary to events in the story, no member of the Indian Corps was ever executed for cowardice on the Western Front. Indeed, its courageous soldiers frequently received the highest awards for gallantry. In short, any factual inaccuracies in the story are mine, not my sources.

The Bhopal Medical Appeal

On the night of 2nd December, 1984, a Union Carbide pesticide plant in Bhopal, India, began leaking twenty-seven tonnes of deadly gas. None of the six safety systems designed to contain such a leak were operational, allowing the gas to spread throughout the city. Half a million people were exposed to the gas and to date, 25,000 people have died as a result of their exposure. More than 120,000 people still suffer from ailments caused by the accident and the subsequent pollution at the plant site.

The Bhopal Medical Appeal funds free medical care at its Sambhavna and Chingari clinics, as well as education and community support for those suffering the effects of the disaster, and to families still being damaged in their thousands by ongoing water poisoning. A percentage of the author's royalties from this book will be donated to the Appeal, so by buying it you are already making a small contribution to its work. If you would like to know more about the Bhopal Medical Appeal, and how you can support it further, please go to: www.bhopal.org

Acknowledgements

This book has been over ten years in the making, during which I have been sustained by the encouragement and expertise of others. My thanks go to the Author's Foundation for a grant which enabled me to write the first draft, and to Hannah Sheppard of HS-LA and Maurice Lyon, who helped me believe that this book might one day find a publisher.

Special thanks go to my editor, Charlie Sheppard, and the team at Andersen Press for taking on the challenge of editing and publishing this book, and to Kim Singh-Sall in the UK, and Guntaas Kaur Chugh in India, for their invaluable insights into the nuances of Indian life and culture.

I am also humbly indebted to those residents of Bhopal whose testimonies were recounted in Indian newspapers following the disaster, and to the Indian soldiers who expressed their experiences of war in their letters home. Echoes of their original, authentic voices can, I hope, be heard in this story.

Finally, I would like to thank my wife Jo and children Jess, Sarah and Sam, for their endless support. Without it, this book would not have found its way to you.